CHUKA

Empty-Grave
Vanilla Edition

by
Richard Jessup

Empty-Grave Publishing

Dear Reader,

Like *The Cincinnati Kid*, this book was adapted to the silver screen; Jessup even wrote the screenplay. I had planned to release a Tango Edition of *CHUKA* but I was unable to confirm the screenplay still exists, let alone get my hands on a copy. Should it ever turn up, you can expect to see a Tango Edition released shortly thereafter.

CHUKA is the second installment of the Richard Jessup Rejuvenation Project—making it official. The rest of Jessup's work will be released over time and my intention is to have just about everything he wrote back in print by 2015. Jessup wrote in multiple genres as well as under a pseudonym and I feel the project should focus first on his diverse writing ability rather than how it evolved over his career—hence, the order of release will not be based on original publication dates. Project information and updates are available at www.RichardJessup.com.

And now I proudly introduce you to a six-chambered man making an against-the-odds stand—the gunfighter known only as—*Chuka!*

A.Nicolai
Empty-Grave
Publishing

empty-grave.com - website
facebook.com/pages/empty-grave-publishing/114806311932977 - facebook
twitter.com/emptygravepub - twitter
feedback@empty-grave.com - comments, concerns, contact

CONTENTS

Chapter One   2

Chapter Two   16

Chapter Three   31

Chapter Four   37

Chapter Five   52

Chapter Six   78

Chapter Seven   88

Chapter Eight   106

Chapter Nine   118

Chapter Ten   127

Chapter Eleven   140

Biography   162

Bibliography   163

His Excellency the Mexican Ambassador
Washington, D.C.

Dear Mr. Ambassador:

Pursuant to your request through the United States Secretary of State for information on the whereabouts of the Mexican citizen, Señorita Helena Chavez, I am enclosing an account of the Indian attack on the U.S. Army Establishment, Fort Clendennon, State of Colorado, U.S.A. on November 17th and 18th, 1876 for forwarding to your government and interested parties.

I beg indulgence of Your Excellency for the delay, but communications and the vast distances traveled by this correspondent to ascertain the facts of the inquiry, justify the lateness. I hasten to assure Your Excellency that, notwithstanding, all speed and every effort has been made for the swift completion of this duty. Sir, I would also beg understanding for omitting certain details of a military nature that in no way add or detract from this narrative account.

Finally, I would like to insert here a note on the ferocity of the attack and the courage of the defense. Undoubtedly, Sir, the Fort Clendennon fight will be placed alongside memorable battles of the past. No man who stood there will go unremembered.

Attacking was a force of more than four hundred and seventy. Defending was a command of thirty troopers, one Sergeant-Major, two Lieutenants, one Captain, one Major, with Colonel Stuart Valois, of Maryland, commanding.

In addition there was an Indian scout, Louis Trent; a stage driver, Earl Baldwin; gun guard, Daniel Howard; Mr. John T. Sheppard, hardware salesman; his wife, Evangeline Sheppard; Señora Veronica Klietz, dueña to Señorita Helena Chavez, the subject of your inquiry; two men, Henry Watkins and Jake Crowford, of Montana country, who were riding north with an infamous gunfighter known only as Chuka . . . .

1

Chapter One

THEY appeared at the top of a small hill a good hour before sundown, a cold and blowing end to a hard day of riding that had never really warmed up, with the wind springing suddenly and causing each to pull hard on his hat. Three of them, their horses blending in with the brown grass of a Colorado November. They paused only briefly at the top of the rise, scanning the flat and deserted stretches on either side of the Trinidad-Granada Trail, marked by twin ruts where stage and freight wagons had scarred the softer spring and summer earth, and saw that nothing moved on the frozen flats below them.

They would not go on to Granada. In another hour or so they would be at Fort Clendennon where they planned to stay the night and then angle off due north the following day. With a nod of his head, the one in the middle, the straight-backed, hard-faced man who rode his horse as if he were part of the animal, with this mouth and eyes tight, and his right hand trailing at his gun butt in a menacing and slightly arrogant readiness, proceeded down the side of the hill, and the others followed, carefully, but with no sign of hesitation as their horses slipped on the frozen ground, and then rode quickly, but not fast, to the trail.

Not long after they had gained the freedom of the road, the middle rider slowed the pace and walked his snorting animal. The other two, a tall, dour, indrawn man with a near frown constantly on his face, the tallest of the three, and an older, middle-aged man with a leathery face who chewed steadily on a tobacco cud while his restless pale eyes betrayed this insouciant action, slowed their horses and matched the pace.

"Toll me the rest of it," middle rider said, moving his right hand in a short commanding gesture. But curiously this gesture also resembled one that an Indian would make in sign language.

The old man chewed reflectively for a long while and then picked up the thread of his story that had been broken when they had automatically quietened, paused and searched the flats on topping the rise. "Well, Sir, Chuka, things happened faster'n they ought after Larrabee came out to the place. Jake here, and me was settin' to digging the yard well. We had been truckin' water in, down and up and over and under from the floor of the place and had set our mind to have it handier, when Larrabee and a half-dozen of his hands kept pace with him right on into the dooryard. It was a purty morning," the older man said thoughtfully. "Spring was high, the last of the snow melt was down to

2

a fair stream through the valley floor and at night I could hear it. The grass was as green as the spackles on a rattler's back in the sun—"

"Get on with it," Chuka said evenly.

"He put it right to us. Said he had the law with him—and he did, Marshall Thorpe was there—and that me and Jake here was under arrest for Half Breed's killing."

"Did you tell 'em?" Chuka asked.

"We told them," the old man said.

"And what did Thorpe say?"

"Larrabee wouldn't let Thorpe talk. By that I mean, he did all the talking, and Larrabee said even if you was the one killed Half Breed, we were there and seen it and he was going to see to it me and Jake here was held just as responsible for it, and he allowed that it was just our word me or Jake didn't kill Half Breed and said you did."

"And that's when you run?" Chuka asked.

"Not right away. I tried to ignore Larrabee and talk directly to Thorpe. Larrabee kept interrupting him and trying to take over, and finally Thorpe got mad as hell and told Larrabee to shut his goddam mouth. I thought Larrabee was going to bust a gut over that, but Thorpe had his dander up by then. I asked Thorpe if he would give me time to try and locate you. Then Larrabee busted in again, saying that he would like to have you come back and hang with me and Jake for the murder of Half Breed."

Chuka turned his head slightly and looked at the older man. His voice was quiet and even. "Larrabee said that, did he?"

"Jake was there. Ask him."

"I believe you," Chuka said mildly.

"Well, go ahead, ask Jake."

"Henry," Chuka said slowly, "I said I believed you."

They rode on in frozen silence a half mile before the conversation started up again. Once more Chuka made the abrupt gesture that looked like an Indian talking sign language. "Go on," he said.

Then Chuka looked at the dour young man at his other side. "What happened after that, Jake? Did Thorpe give you time to try and locate me?"

3

"Yeah," Jake said. "We wrote to a bunch of places, most of the summer. Dodge City, San Antonio. We talked to people passing through and asked about you."

"I didn't know," Chuka said, "or I would have come."

"We know that," Jake said.

"I just wanted you to hear me say it," Chuka replied easily.

"When we didn't get no response from all the writing and asking, Larrabee, who had been held in check all this time by Thorpe, began to make noises again. Big noises — in town."

"And you say the only burr under his tail was Half Breed's killing?" Chuka asked.

"That's what he wanted everybody to believe. But you know the people up around our country. They never did like Larrabee," Henry said. "We found out later though."

"We sure did," Jake said sourly. "Right damn quick."

"What was it?"

"Just wanted our place, that's all," Henry said meanly.

"And he intended using Half Breed's killing to get you out of the way?" Chuka asked.

"That's the way of it," Henry said.

"What did Thorpe have to say about this? I know him for a fair man. Least he always appeared so to me."

Jake and Henry looked at each other. "Let me get back to it, back to where Thorpe came out during the late summer and asked us if we had heard anything from you. We said we hadn't. Then Thorpe said he wasn't going to sit still for Larrabee doing things like this and went into town that very afternoon to tell Larrabee it was finished. That night, Thorpe was shot down."

Chuka looked sideways at Henry. "That so?" He said softly.

"No one knew anything about it."

Chuka rode on silently for a few minutes. "And —?" he said finally, easing his weight in the saddle.

"Well, Larrabee took that damn Cheyenne lawyer of his'n, the one they call Corky, and rode over to the territory seat and pulled a few

4

old red noses and came back with a new lawman. All his'n. Wrapped up an delivered. Dawson, the new lawman, made tracks for our place, backed up by Larrabee's guns. We got wind of it and lit out."

"Before talking to this Dawson?" Chuka asked.

Jake and Henry looked at each other again.

"Well?" Chuka demanded.

Neither of the men said anything. Chuka suddenly pulled up on the leather and stopped the horse in the middle of the trail. He eyed them both as they stopped to look at him. "You're leaving something out of this aren't you?"

He did not miss the look that passed between them. "Well?" He demanded.

When neither of them answered, Chuka stood up in the stirrups and stretched his legs. "It's November. And I'm cold. I owe you something, both of you, for what you did for me back in Montana. You didn't have to take me in that time."

"Listen, Chuka—" Henry said.

"No you listen," Chuka said. "I owe you. And I'm willing to pay off, but—"

Chuka never finished. The sudden whip and snap and hoarse cry from the oncoming stage, rattling along the trail from Trinidad to Granada, with a night stop-over at Clendennon, broke down on them from the rear.

"Heeeeeeeyaaaaaa!" The driver's cry alerted them and the three riders moved off the trail to watch the Lipton coach swing past them, the gun guard ready, carbine up, the driver whipping the teams. They caught only a glimpse of the passengers inside the coach as it passed them, tearing down the road in a dead line for Clendennon. The noise and the rush of the snorting horses beyond them, the three riders drifted back into the middle of the trail and looked after the vanishing coach. They started after it, moving easily, a little faster; but not so fast they couldn't talk.

"Chuka, me and Jake talked a long time about this before we come looking for you. And what we did for you back in Montana, well, you don't owe."

"I came in shot up and with a fever. You took me in and saved my hide from rotting out in the open," Chuka said, with a pleasant protest in his voice. "So I'm beholden to you. But you're leaving something out of this, ain't you? Both of you?"

When neither of them replied, Chuka spoke again. "I would hate to go back with you and find out things that are different from what you been telling me."

"You think we lying?" Jake asked sharply.

"Now Jake," Chuka said easily, "I didn't say that."

Jake dug his heels into the pony. The animal skittered ahead. "I'll go on to Clendennon and let 'em know we're coming in," he said over his shoulder; and then he was gone, the hoofbeats on the hard ground fading in the cold.

"Well, you might as well know," Henry said, watching his young partner, "because you would have found out anyway."

Chuka waited. Then he spoke softly. "You fought the new lawman, Dawson," he said, making it a statement.

Henry jerked his head around. He looked at Chuka. "I might have known that you'd figure it out."

"Wasn't any other reason for you to run. So far, you and Jake was on one side of the law, and Larrabee on the other, with the law neutral. What happened?"

Henry's voice settled into a hardness that had not been evident before. "Dawson said we were under arrest for killing Half Breed, I asked him if he had a warrant. He just laughed. Larrabee laughed. We had a hundred and seventy seven head of cows, more than enough to sell off and pay the taxes. I saw through it right away. We go to jail and then someone takes the herd, the place goes bad for taxes and Larrabee's got what he wanted in the first place. Looking back, I can see that was all he planned with Thorpe. Just to get us out of the way so he could get to us without any trouble. Well, Jake saw through it too. He was in the house. When he heard the last words said between me and Larrabee and Dawson, and saw that it was the end of talking, Jake, well, he pulled out that carbine of his'n with them big grained shells and started popping 'em off. You should have seen them scatter." Henry shook his head. "I tried to stop him, but it was too late. Larrabee was hit, bad, but not too bad, and Dawson was dead. Couple of the others were hit, then they scattered. We didn't even wait around. We just went out to the back and got the horses ready, took what little money we had and the papers on the place and that's when we ran out."

Chuka was silent until they had dropped over the top of a rise. In the distance they could see Clendennon. "I haven't seen any posters out on either of you."

"Well, that doesn't mean there isn't any," Henry said.

"Is that all of it?"

"Every gospel."

"And you started looking for me?" Chuka asked.

"One place after another," Henry said. "It wasn't hard to get a line on you; but you sure do travel fast."

Chuka allowed himself a faint smile. "I still don't see," he said, the smile fading, "what you want me to do."

"Well, I don't rightly know either, Chuka," Henry said slowly. "Jake killed Dawson and that's not lie."

"Did you ever find out if Dawson actually had a warrant?"

"What difference would that make?" Henry asked.

"It might help us," Chuka said slowly, "when we get back up there."

The us did not escape Henry. "I've thought it over and over and over, Chuka, since we've been looking for you. It looks to me and Jake done skinned ourselves and there ain't no way to back out of it." His voice, for the first time, was spiritless.

"We'll see," Chuka said at length. "Come'n, let's get on into Clendennon. I'm damn near frozen to this saddle."

The two riders tightened their hats and ducked their faces into the collars of their fleece jackets and broke the wind in a headlong plunge for the stockade, now deep purple in the last of the sun's rays.

* * *

In the very special world of Louis Trent, a man walked with death as a boon companion, laughing at him, taking care that he did not come too close. It was the only way if you wanted to enter the big country—a land stretching from the Canadian timber line south to the Rio Grande, a country of Twin Buttes, Tetons, Devil's Hole, Stake Plains, of deep valley country in Wyoming and Montana with grass as high as knuckles of a full grown buffalo, and a country of sweetened streams when lazing on a mossy bank was important to a man and a day could be passed just listening to the interwoven recital of birds, a land to be blessed by a soft mountain breeze, or licked hot by a duster on the Nebraska flatlands, where weeks would pass without seeing another living human, many dead ones—but few live ones. Louis Trent had known it when it was a pure country, virgin pure, scented with the fragrance of valley honeysuckle so strong a man could get sick of smelling it. He had spent a lifetime in this special world, as a boy, as a youth, as a man, Indian fighter, mountain man, trapping along the beaver streams when beaver was important, turning to buffalo hides when beaver trickled out of style. Louis Trent has scouted the country from one end to the other, spread-eagle over the whole length and breadth of it. And then his private place (for every man that entered upon that big country considered it his own) began to shrink, shortening its lines, its length and its breadth. Louis Trent was confined to the grassy tablelands of eastern Colorado, a new state in the Union, about ninety days old. So much had changed. But one thing remained the same: death was still the companion to be wary of and to laugh at.

As Trent gazed out over the dying grass on the tableland country, seeing it through a gun notch just off the south sally port at Fort Clendennon, his ear cocked for the sounds of horses as much as his eyes searched the bending trail, he rolled through his mind thoughts of the big country, idling along nearly fifty years of his life—the good times and the hard times—all of them softer now with the passing of time. He was summing up his life, and it was late, and he had not put much by for his keep when he couldn't make his own meat. A man would have been a fool to live for tomorrow in that country in that time. But it was here. The time had come. He would have to think seriously about these things; and then he pushed them out of his mind. He had a fat winter coming up at Fort Clendennon. He could think about it anytime during the long snow-in at the Fort. And then he grinned, a nearly toothless snicker, as he recognized that he could not change a lifetime of habit. He had always put things off. Just because he was getting old, it was no different. But deep within him, Louis Trent knew he would have to make a decision this winter.

The arrival of the Trinidad-Granada stage pushed his thoughts to one side. The six-horse Lipton coach bucked and rocked as it traveled the last thousand yards up the five percent grade to the entrance. Behind him Trent could hear the guards and the tower sentry shouting orders to open the gates. There was a rush of hooves as the stage swept in to be greeted by a brooding silence from the troopers. There would be no mail on the up-run from Trinidad. The mail came down from Granada at the railhead. Good things came down from Granada. Only tired and weary travelers could be expected on the up-run. Trent swept

8

his eyes across the brown plains that stretched to a rocky nest a mile away, saw nothing and hurried from the sally port to view the new arrivals. But before the coach stopped swinging there was a yell from the post on the north tower.

"Ho! Rider approaching."

Trent automatically swung around to see, and then as a lone rider beat it toward the Fort, he saw a pair of riders pounding down the trail.

Three of them. He grunted. Hard tails, range bums picking up a free meal and a hay stall for the night. He dismissed the approaching riders and turned once more to watch the passengers alight from the stage. He saw only that there were three women and a drummer, and then the first of the riders whipped into the Fort followed closely by the pair. Trent swung around to look at them.

Chuka!

The name exploded inside the old scout's head like a cannon shot as he watched the man pull up his pony and ease down to the ground. Trent forgot about the others the moment the big man appeared.

Chuka—Trent was hardly able to restrain himself. His eyes traveled the full measure of the man standing beside his horse. A shade over six feet, a sheep fleece jacket, Cheyenne chaps, he looked mean and there was a hardness about him. A well-kept blue steel .44 Frontier Colt hung low on the gunfighter's right leg and was tied down over whipcord trousers. Trent's eyes lingered on the gun and holster. The gun was bright and clean with what looked like an eight inch barrel; the holster was the opposite, old and scratched. Trent could see it must be as hard as saddle leather. Gun leather. A holster that would never drag a man's draw.

Chuka. There was cruelty in the man's face, too. Trent saw that at once. Lou Trent had seen a great deal of cruelty in his lifetime and for him it was easy to read it in a man's face. Everything about Chuka was wrong. A hard case, Trent thought, and all wrong. Dead wrong.

Quickly, so he could get back to Chuka, the old scout sized up the two companions. One a tall, slow and deliberate man, with a way about him that spelled caution to Trent, and an older man, not too much younger than Trent himself, who looked as if he might have been through some of it—then back to Chuka, where his real interest and curiosity lay. Unmoved, leaning against a post, Trent followed the three with his eyes as Sergeant-Major Hahnsbach escorted them to Colonel Valois' office for official and formal permission to stay the night at the Fort.

Then the old scout frowned. Everything was wrong—except something didn't quite add up. Something there didn't belong with the rest of it.

It was some time before the old man was able to pinpoint the thing that disturbed him. And it wasn't until he had gone back in his mind, gone back in time to Dodge City, to the one other time he had seen Chuka. It had been the face of a younger man then. Softer. And the cruelty that was now apparent in the face of the man had been just a go-to-hell wildness. But nobody to Trent's knowledge could handle a gun in quite the same way. Trent chewed on it for several hours after the arrival of the stage before he hit upon it. It was the gunfighter's eyes, Trent thought. They were black and they looked straight at you; but they were *soft* eyes. It just didn't fit the hardness in the face.

Chuka. That was all the name Lou Trent had ever heard. But it was enough, and the man was in Fort Clendennon.

Not long afterward, the weak November sun dropped and the cold winds came down from the Colorado mountains to wash over the table country.

The harvest moon came up over the frozen grasslands like a silver lantern and cast pale cold light on the dying, retrenching land as hard winter bore down from the Rockies to the staked plains. Fort Clendennon lay halfway between Trinidad and Granada. At Granada, on the Kansas line, travelers left the short-line stage and caught the train for the east and west. With the coming of winter, the prospect of being isolated in Trinidad chased those who did not have to stay. For several weeks now the stage had been hauling passengers and light freight to the railhead and returning empty, except for the mail. Trent knew this would be one of the last, if not the last, stage to come through. Winter was coming early and it would not be long before the trail was choked with snow. The only way in or out of Trinidad or Fort Clendennon would be by saddle bronc, and mail, if there was any, would pile up at the railroad, and wait for the clear weather.

At the first darkness after the arrival of the stage, Trent sat at his post. Now with the first light of the moon, he patrolled the watch, moving from one tower to another, personally inspecting each man's rifle, his restless eyes never stopping in their sweep over the frost-covered, hardening land. At the north tower the largest and tallest at Clendennon, he stood with a trooper and studied the deep, level grass country of eastern Colorado and the route that Hanu would take when the old Arapaho Chief broke his summer camp in Rush Creek and started the

10

southward trek to the Red River watershed and the site of the Arapaho winter lodges. Once Hanu had made his move, Trent could then relax for the winter and think about the future.

The future. An annoying idea for Louis Trent. And he could not shake it. Change for him was more than just having the Indians cowed, or the land filling up with the people, or having Colorado a state in the Union. There were other changes. There was a civilization advancing on him. One with order and justice. Already the Colorado countries were putting up their own sheriffs and not relaying on the territorial marshal. With each country holding its own sheriff, Trent swore, men like himself were being hemmed in. And men like Chuka were going to have to go. And Fort Clendennon had been a part of the establishment of that coming order and justice. The army was there to maintain peace with the settlers as well as the old Hanu's Arapaho.

The Fort was beginning to settle into sleep. The last card in the last hand in the squad room game was being played, the singing stopped, the last horse settled in the stables. The only sound in the Fort now, aside from the barking of the pet dog fox the troopers kept in a cage, were the laughter and the general merrymaking coming from the officer's mess where Colonel Valois was entertaining the travelers.

Trent reviewed these people slowly, examining each detail as he remembered it. Earl Baldwin, the driver of the stage, a sinewy big-handed man who could drive a six-horse Lipton coach faster and with more control than Trent had ever seen; Dan Howard, the gun guard, not always used on the stage, a range hand from around Trinidad who took the extra job when money or important freight was being shipped down from Granada to Clendennon, or on to Trinidad; Sheppard, a hardware drummer on his way back east after a summer long trek through the big country, moving from community to community, selling his axes, plows, nails, guns, carbines, shells and with him; Mrs. Sheppard, a saloon babe Trent had seen in Trinidad. She had worked in the Casino and now, very obviously, was trading off her favors for a ticket out of Trinidad. Both Mr. and Mrs. Sheppard were half drunk when they got off the stage. Señorita Chavez, a Spanish Mexican lady of quality, with bright and shining eyes staring at everything and missing nothing as she worked her shawl against the wind, and with her, a hard-nosed dueña, rasping, shrill voiced woman, her Spanish thick with the sounds of her Austrian background. Señora Klietz, Trent thought, rolling the unlikely name over in his mind. One of the leftovers from the Mexican court of Maximilian, and then the three riders, Jake Crowford and Henry Watkins—and finally there was Chuka.

Trent saw them all in his mind as they had gotten off the stage or ridden in, and he turned now to stare out over the parade grounds to the row of lantern lights along the gallery outside the mess where the party was still going on. Unconsciously Trent reached down and worked on the heavy knot in his right thigh. Feeling around the hard edge of a Sioux arrowhead, he cursed for the thousandth time the decision by the Army doctors to leave the arrowhead in his leg, their explanation being the missile had found a seat in his thigh and it was thought better to leave it alone. The leg had gradually stiffened on him so that a pronounced limp had developed, and winter always brought on added pain and misery.

At ten P.M. Trent climbed down from his watch on the catwalk of the near and distant flats in the dark but moonlit night and limped to his bed, found a small flat bottle of whiskey and slipped it inside his jacket. He returned to the watch and made a circle of the Fort, eyes never stopping in their sweep of the dark and brooding land before him.

Fort Clendennon, Trent thought, working on his leg, trying to get the circulation back into it—Fort Hell, Fort Blood, Fort Death—all names used by the troopers assigned to Colonel Valois' command; but not without reason, good reason. The toughs, the rebels, the guardhouse bullies, the near cowards, gamblers, thieves, and even alleged murderers who had all stood trial and been acquitted, they were the men who made up the military body of Clendennon. And the officers were not much better than their men—drunks, gamblers, cruel or stupid, or both, whose offenses were not quite enough to prompt dismissal, and like their troops, were unfit for service in any command except Clendennon. Lonely and isolated, the Fort was set broad and open and unprotected in the grasslands and commanded the area fifty-four miles south of Granada and fifty miles north of Trinidad. A trooper caught outside the Fort at night stood little chance against the roving bands of Cheyenne renegades, or Hanu's Arapaho, or the drifting, slave-taking, cruel Comanches. And even experience did not always guarantee a safe return to the protection of the Fort. There was a small but growing cemetery and it stood as mute testimony to this fact. Yet there had been troopers that tried to desert and make it alone across the grass country rather than face the harsh discipline of Valois, and of the few that made it to Trinidad or Granada, every man had been returned to Clendennon where his life then became a living hell.

And for those that died, there was a shipment of replacements, twice monthly. One, two, three, even four men from all posts across the country were picked up in Granada by sergeant-Major Hahnsbach

12

who actually, physically, brought the soldiers into line, as often with his ham-like fists as with his roaring voice of authority. It was seldom, indeed, that Sergeant Hahnsbach faced a problem with the men of Clendennon that he could not handle himself and needed to bring to the attention of Colonel Valois.

The men either died in Clendennon or they were returned to other commands. No one came back. Once there, they wanted no more of it.

The restoration of men was only one-half of the original purpose of setting up still another fort in the area. There were five major Army forts within a hundred-fifty mile radius: Fort Bascom to the south, Fort Garland to the west, Fort Wallace to the north, Fort Hays, northeast and Fort Dodge due east. Fort Clendennon, in its four years of existence had broken up the larger, more organized bands of Cheyenne, Arapaho and Comanches and offered protection to the settlers. But there were just as many memories for the Indians as for the settlers in the four years that Valois had swept them back, and Lou Trent recognized the threat of a showdown between Hanu's Arapaho, the strongest camp left in Colorado, and Fort Clendennon.

Most of the summer, Trent had been watching and checking on the ragged, unattached groups of Apache, Comanches, Cheyenne, Arapaho, some Sioux and Ute that Hanu had welcomed to his lodges at Rush Creek. It was near the time for Hanu to make his move. Lou Trent did not for one moment believe that the force of three hundred lodges, numbering more than four hundred braves with a thirst for revenge in their hearts, would break camp and pass on into the southern plains without a try at Clendennon.

An attack was in the wind. Trent had been making his reports to Valois all summer, who in turn had taken Trent's information to higher command. But the commanding officers at Wallace and Garland paid it no mind.

"Hanu wouldn't dare," the General had said. "With Wallace, Hays, Garland, Bascom and Dodge so close by, not a chance, Colonel Valois. If we thought it was serious, do you think we would leave you down there with thirty or forty men, most of whom couldn't be depended on in a fight anyway? No Sir, Colonel. Your scout is wagging you."

But everything the old scout knew to be facts pointed to an attack. The temper of the Indians, the memory of Washita and the crushing defeat of the Cheyenne, the recent statehood of Colorado putting Arapaho County, as it was once known, further out of their reach. And most important to the old scout was the news of the defeat of Custer, who had taken part in

13

Washita and, along with his men, had been slaughtered by the Sioux at Little Big Horn. All were signs not be misread by the old scout.

Something was going to happen and it would be a miracle if it didn't, Trent concluded to himself, staring out over the dark frozen wastes. Since the middle of the summer when the news of Custer's slaughter had reached the Hanu camp, the word of that disaster coming swiftly as if carried on the wind, the build-up had begun. And now it was time for the Arapaho to pick up and move to their winter lodges five hundred miles to the southeast.

It was nearly one o'clock in the morning when Trent, only half listening to the continuing party in the officers' mess, grunted to himself, took a long pull on the whiskey and made a decision. He slipped down from the north tower, jumping lightly to the ground and hurried to the stables. Once inside, he turned up the lantern and went directly to his horse and began to saddle up. Suddenly he whirled around. "Who's there!"

"Ease off," a flat, even voice responded.

"Come out in the light," Trent demanded, relieved by the voice and the English to know that it wasn't a brave from Hanu's camp.

The shadows in the deep side of the stable shifted. Then the man appeared, almost as if he were a shadow himself.

"Chuka—!" the scout said.

The tall man moved in on him, his eyes bore down. "Who are you?"

"Lou Trent, post scout."

"You going out to scout now?" Chuka asked. "It's one in the morning."

"Of course I'm going out now. When you want me to go? Twelve o'clock noon?"

"You're a damn fool," Chuka said.

"Ain't you heard about old Hanu and his build up?"

Chuka stood a moment watching Trent saddle a roan, then without a word or a sound, turned and moved back into the shadows.

"What are you doing here, mister?" Trent demanded.

"Seeing to my horse."

"At one o'clock in the morning? You're a damn fool."

Chuka turned his head slightly and looked up at the old man. "You got a lot of mouth."

14

"I'd think a hard case like you would be inside whooping it up with the Colonel and the ladies."

"The ladies went to bed. Mrs. Sheppard is the only one whooping it up," Chuka said.

The horse was saddled. Trent began to check his guns, both carbine and six-gun. Then he examined his knife.

Chuka watched him, leaning against a post, smoking.

Trent took the leather and started to lead his horse out the door. "Don't set the place on fire, Chuka," Trent said.

"If I don't, how will you know how to get back?"

"Jest smell you out."

"Lot of mouth—for an old man."

Trent stopped at the door. His hand swept down and up in one easy move. The knife whistled through the air and caught the post a few inches away from Chuka's head.

Chuka reached up and pulled the knife out and hefted it, feeling for balance. He flipped the knife into the ground at Trent's feet. "Lot of mouth. And tough."

"I'll do, sonny," Trent said. "I been doing a long time." He swung into the saddle. Chuka walked to the door after him.

"Adios," Trent said, swinging toward the gate.

"Good luck," Chuka said in the same flat voice that never varied in tone or pitch.

The small one-horse gate at the side of the larger one was swung open and the scout disappeared into the night.

Chuka was walking toward the officer's mess when he heard the post call. Soft and quiet in the dark cold night.

"Post one—all's well."

"Post two—all's well."

"Post three—all's well."

"Sergeant of the guard! All posts—quiet on the watch!"

The harvest moon was high, racing across the sky. The wind had died to a bone rattling, deadening cold.

15

Chapter Two

"AHHH! Mr. Chuka rejoins us. How goes the night, Mr. Chuka?" Colonel Stuart Valois' voice curled with a fine shade of sarcasm.

Chuka returned the greeting with a faint, charming smile. "Cold."

Chuka slid one of the chairs away from the table and moved closer to the stove. He did not actually turn his back on the tight informal group around the table, but it was clear that he no longer wanted to be included in the general conversation. Yet he could still see what was going on.

Two lieutenants, one very young, not more than twenty-one, with a weak chin, and one very old, with watery eyes betraying him as a drunk, had settled themselves into a half nodding, half drunken sleep at the side of the table. The Captain had left the mess early. Valois, Sheppard and his wife Evangeline, along with Major Cook, a tall man with chin whiskers and hard eyes, remained seated at the table. Sheppard was so drunk he could hardly keep himself in his chair. If Valois was drunk, which Chuka did not believe, it was a curious kind of drunk. The man had not changed since they sat down to supper at seven P.M. Major Cook drank steadily and showed nothing of the whiskey's effect at all. He sat quietly smoking long cigars and responding to Valois only when spoken to directly. Evangeline Sheppard sat upright, her face flushed, wisps of hair ragged on her temples. She twirled a half-filled glass of whiskey and now and then would lift it to her lips for a half-swallow and then appear to hold it, allowing the drink to ease down her throat. Señorita Chavez and Señora Klietz had retired from the meal immediately after eating. Jake and Henry, along with the stage driver and gun guard had taken a few drinks and then had left the mess when Hahnsbach came to show them their bunks with the troops.

"Cold," Valois repeated. "The night is cold."

Chuka said nothing. He raised his boot and stuck the heel in the grill around the stove. No one said anything for a full minute.

"Do you know, Mrs. Sheppard," Valois said slowly, "that you are being treated to a questionable opportunity?"

Out of the corner of his eye, Chuka saw the woman raise her head.

"Yes, Madame, it is a rare privilege."

"What's that, Colonel?" Evangeline Sheppard asked.

Chuka noted that her speech was thickening.

"If I may be so bold, Madame, perhaps you will be fortunate enough to have children and I dare say that one night, in the years to come, you will describe a cold night on the Colorado tablelands when you sat down to meat and drink with—" Valois paused and looked around the room, "a notorious gambler in Army circles." His eyes came to rest on Major Cook.

"A gambler. What's so unusual about that?"

"Unusual, Madame, in that when Major Cook dealt the cards, cards, my dear Mrs. Sheppard, appeared from every unlikely place you can imagine. Of course I never saw the Major play, but I have it on pretty good authority that cards appeared from his sleeve, from the bottom of the deck, from his vest. But no one, to this day, has seen him deal from the top of the deck."

Valois paused. "Is that not so, Major Cook?"

Cook did not reply. He dropped his eyes and flipped the ash from his cigar.

"*I asked you a question, Sir.*"

Major Cook stood. "Permission to be excused, Sir."

"Permission denied. Sit down, Major Cook. Answer my question."

Major Cook sat down. His neck was stiff, his back straight. Chuka saw that his hands were shaking slightly.

"I was a gambler, yes, Sir."

"That is a statement. It is not the answer to my question."

"I'm not sure of the question, Sir."

"Has anyone ever seen you deal from the top of a deck? That is the question."

Major Cook swallowed. Chuka spun around in his chair and watched from the far side of the room. "Yes, Sir," Cook said.

"*Who* saw you?"

"It would be impossible to say, at this moment, Sir."

"*Where* did this alleged top dealing take place?"

Cook stood again. "Sir, I am not well. I request permission to be excused."

"Sit down, Major Cook. Your answer is vague and evasive. I don't believe you have ever dealt a hand of cards from the top of the deck."

"Sir, I request permission to be— "

"*Sit down!*" Valois said tightly. "Permission is denied."

Major Cook sat down. His hands were shaking so hard he could hardly pick up his drink.

Valois turned to Evangeline Sheppard. "You see? A rare opportunity, Madame."

Evangeline Sheppard picked up her head. "Yes, Colonel Valois—"

"*Lieutenant Mack!*"

The young officer snapped up drunkenly. He stared, mumbled something, then turned half around in his chair and put his head to rest on the table. Valois walked hurriedly around to the officer, picked up a pitcher of water and poured it over the man's head. "Lieutenant Mack!"

"Uh—ah—Sir— "

"*Attention!*"

Mack struggled to his feet. "Sir?"

Valois replaced the pitcher on the table and walked back to his chair. He sat down, hooking one leg over his chair arm. "This officer, Mrs. Sheppard, only ten months out of West Point, was attached to a company in New York City. Strange things began to happen to the belongings of the men. Would you believe it, Madame, this young officer, trained to be a gentleman, educated to be an officer in the United States Army—was a *thief!*"

"Please, Colonel," Evangeline Sheppard said softly. She turned to her husband. She shook him. "Johnny—Johnny, it's time we leave."

"Oh, stay Madame," Valois said gently. He put his arm on Evangeline's chair and held it down firmly. "Lieutenant Mack—"

"Sir?"

"How much money did you steal from your own troops, officers included?"

"Sir—I ah—"

"*How much*, lieutenant Mack?"

"I don't recall, sir."

"You *can* recall, if I ask you to, Sir. And I am asking you to tell me how much you stole from your own officers and men!"

Silence.

"Well, Lieutenant, are you counting in your head?"

"Nearly four thousand dollars, Sir."

Valois turned to Evangeline. "Think of that—in ten months. And this had to be done slyly, Madame. Only at night, when the men were sleeping. Lieutenant Mack would then slip into their quarters and rifle their money and valuables."

"Sir, I would like to remind you that my family returned the money. There was no loss."

Valois turned to Evangeline. "That is true, there was no loss. He comes from one of the finest families in Boston." Valois turned back to Mack. "But there was a loss Lieutenant. The four years that you spent at West Point, your training, the money the government and the people of this country spent to educate you, that was a loss, wasn't it, Sir?"

Chuka saw the young man straighten.

"I am still on duty, Sir."

"Oh, yes, I had forgotten that your family pulled every string in Washington, D.C. to keep you from being sent to prison and keep you in service until you could resign with honor. What is the price of honor, Mack? What did it cost your family to save you from prison?"

"Sir, I cannot answer that question."

"Is honor sacrifice?"

"Sir—"

"Is honor a courageous death?"

"Colonel Valois, Sir—"

"Don't make any statements to me, Lieutenant Mack. I would like to know your answer as to what, what exactly, is the price of honor?"

"There is no price, Sir, ultimately."

"But your family paid for your honor. So a price was agreed on and paid. Therefore, Lieutenant Mack, you are a man without honor."

Silence.

"Would you disagree, Lieutenant Mack?"

"No, Sir."

"You may sit down," Valois said. He turned to Evangeline. John Sheppard somehow had managed to come awake and had heard the last of the exchange.

"I think we had better call it a night, Eve," Sheppard said. "That ride on up to Granada is going to be hard enough without getting too little sleep."

"Yes," Evangeline said.

"Well, Madame, will you remember this night?"

Evangeline Sheppard turned and looked at her husband. "Yes, Colonel Valois."

The door opened a moment before the Sheppards rose from the table. Sergeant Otto Hahnsbach, a huge man with a barrel chest, took three steps inside and came to attention. "Beg pardon, Colonel, Sir."

"What is it, Sergeant? Has one of your troopers deserted on a cold night like this?"

"No, Sir. No desertions, Sir. But the scout has just left the Fort. I thought the Colonel would like to know."

"Where is Captain Carrol?"

"In his quarters, I believe, Sir."

"Did he tell you to report to me?"

"No, Sir, Colonel—that is—"

"Don't try to cover for the man, Sergeant," Valois said.

"Yes, Sir. I wasn't trying to do nothing like that, Sir."

"You were, Sergeant, but it is an admirable trait in a trooper. Admirable, that is, in a man who has not a single blemish on his record."

"Thank you, Sir," Hahnsbach said. "But—"

"Tell Captain Carrol I wish to see him at once."

"Yes, Sir." Sergeant Otto Hahnsbach saluted, executed a perfect about-face and exited from the room.

John Sheppard rose from the table and helped his wife. "Well, Colonel Valois, I want to thank you for a most enjoyable evening. It has been a long time indeed."

20

"Mrs. Sheppard, ma'am I bid you good night."

"Thank you, Colonel," Evangeline Sheppard replied, glancing at her husband as the Colonel lifted her hand to his lips.

"Mr. Sheppard, no doubt your lovely wife will tell you of this evening, when you were—ah—in your cups, Sir."

Sheppard said nothing.

"I'm afraid I may have shocked her with revelations about the past of some of my officers," Valois said, not moving and giving no indication that he was going to let the Sheppards leave either.

Sheppard was determined to go and he stepped around Valois, taking his wife's hand and leading her toward the door. They had no sooner gained the entrance when the door opened and a short, thickset man with an absolutely bald head appeared, his clothes in such disarray it was obvious to all that he had dressed hastily.

With the appearance of the man, Sheppard took his wife and pulled her back away from the door. Immediately behind the new arrival, Otto Hahnsbach stood at attention.

"You sent for me, Sir?" The man said.

"Captain Carrol, are you not the officer of the watch?"

"I am, Sir."

"Did you know there was a rider that left the post?"

"If you mean Lou Trent, Sir, he told me he was thinking about taking another look around outside to see if any of Hanu's braves were around."

"*If* I mean Trent. *Of course I mean Trent!*" Valois said. "Why wasn't this fact reported to me?"

"He had not yet left the post, Colonel. I left it up to him. You know how it is with scouts, Sir. They don't like to talk about what they're going to do."

"Is the fact that the only scout on the post leaves in the middle of the night on a dangerous mission not an important military fact, Captain Carrol?"

"It could be judged a fact, Colonel."

"An important fact!" Valois insisted. "That the commander should know about at once. Such information should come from the duty officer and not left to chance for an enlisted soldier to see, judge, decide on the relevant value of what he has seen, and then take it upon himself to report it to the commanding officer."

Captain Carrol remained silent.

John Sheppard used this moment of silence to ease forward, holding Evangeline's hand, stepping to the door.

Valois stepped forward as if he did not see them, slammed the door and leaned on it.

"Turn around, Captain Carrol."

The Captain turned and remained at attention. Valois looked at Evangeline Sheppard. "Madame, one more study for your memory of this night. The display of incompetence by Captain Carrol is just one more to be added to a long record of consistent neglect of duty." Valois paused and sighed. "Would you believe it, Mrs. Sheppard, this man still considers himself a soldier? Still insists that he wants nothing so much as to be returned to duty on another post and have the past forgotten? A man that has his record of neglect. Well! It is not my place to dismiss an officer from the United States Army."

Valois walked to the table and picked up a glass. He did not drink, but turned and looked at Carrol. "How long ago was it, Captain?"

"How long ago was what, Sir?"

"That moment when you buckled under pressure, Captain Carrol, and let thirty-six men die. Buckled under pressure—that was your defense, wasn't it? Complaining that you had not slept for nearly three days."

"It was not a complaint, Sir. It was a fact."

"It was a fact, also, Captain Carrol, that you let thirty-six men die! And they had not slept for nearly three days either!"

Captain Carrol looked Colonel Valois in the eye. His jaw tightened. "Colonel Valois, I resent your—"

"Resent what, Captain? That I simply state the record?"

"Resent your airing my record," he glanced at the Sheppards, "publicly, Sir."

"Mr. and Mrs. She are taxpaying citizens of this country, and it is your sworn duty to protect them. And civilians know little enough about the ways and habits of the Army not to be allowed a peek inside when the opportunity arises."

Sheppard cleared his throat. "Colonel, I would just as soon let it go," he said, his breath rasping.

"Of *course*! I'm so sorry, Sir. And Mrs. Sheppard. Of course, I'll let it go."

Valois stepped to the door and started to open it.

"But *I'd* like to hear more, Colonel. I'm a taxpaying citizen," Chuka said from the corner near the stove. "Got any more broken-down brass you want to trot out?"

Valois froze with his hand on the door. The room was absolutely still. Carrol and Hahnsbach did not move a muscle. Lieutenant Mack and Lieutenant Daly, at his side, were still. Major Cook turned his head slowly. The Sheppards stepped away from the door, drawing clear to the back of the room.

Valois walked halfway back into the room and looked down at Chuka, who had not moved. The two men looked at each other. Finally Valois dropped his hand on the shoulder of Lieutenant Daly. "Lieutenant Daly here was tried for rape—and—acquitted, of course. Would you like to hear about him?"

Chuka shifted his feet on the stove, spit accurately and listened to the spittle sizzle. "Well, I'll tell you Colonel, I'd like to hear *Daly* tell it."

"Tell the taxpayer, Lieutenant," Valois said, not taking his eyes away from Chuka, and speaking in a soft, pleasant voice.

Daly cleared his throat, but he said nothing.

"Tell him, Lieutenant." Valois said again, easily.

The voice of Lieutenant Daly was like that of a man saying his last prayer. He began to sweat. "Sir—"

"Tell him, Mike," Valois said softly, patting the man on the shoulder.

"I was on leave," Daly began. "I had been on duty, posted at Fort Kiley, Texas. The Comanches were raiding. I took a patrol out one night, and we were ambushed, and I was the only one to escape. I was wounded in the shoulder and returned to the post hospital. After the shoulder healed up a bit, I was given a pass for the afternoon. And— and after being cooped up in the hospital for so long, I decided to ride out and find out about one of the families that had been hit by the Comanches."

"You're making it too nice, Mike," Valois said again. "Hurry up and get to the part where—"

"Let him tell it, Colonel," Chuka said easily, but in the same flat, even voice.

Daly looked at Chuka. He licked his lips. "I hadn't gone far on my ride, but was well out in the country, when I heard gunfire. I circled and came upon the scene of the conflict. There were about a dozen Comanche bucks, they had already killed the men and were sneaking up on the house. There was one gun still firing. The Comanches circled the house, broke in from the back, and in a minute came out the front. They had a woman with them. I had my pistol, but I knew there was little chance. With my arm in a sling and so painful it even hurt to ride, I could only hope to get a maximum of six of them."

Daly paused, suddenly reached out and drank half a glass of whiskey. He wiped his lips. "But I rode in anyway, holding my fire until I could make sure. I was lucky. They didn't see me until I was halfway in, and by that time I saw there was a chance. A carbine had been dropped on the ground during the fight—and their—attentions to the—woman—and I stopped short of my ride clear in, gained possession of the carbine and forted up behind a wagon. I got four of them—"

Daly took another drink. The room was a deadening, humming silence. The rasping voice of Daly, who was speaking in a low, hoarse whisper, seemed loud and clear.

"Then they saw it was only one man. They pulled the woman and their wounded back into the house and just kept up a fire. Enough to keep me pinned down, not really trying to get at me, I'll never know why—"

"Neither will anyone else, Mike," Valois said.

Daly jumped up. "Damn you!" He roared. "It happened just the way I'm telling it."

Hahnsbach was in back of the Lieutenant in a split second. But the fury of Daly's outburst was spent as soon as he had spoken. Valois, Chuka noted, had not moved. He had not flinched.

"They drew off at night. I went in, finally. She was there—still alive—I don't know why they didn't kill her—but they didn't. She was unconscious—"

Daly paused. "I went to her, picked her up and tried, as best I could with my shoulder, to get her to a bed. She woke up, started screaming and fighting. She was a heavy woman and by then my shoulder was giving me more pain than I could take. She scratched my face and nearly put out one of my eyes. When she hit my shoulder a blow, I

24

dropped her. And I remember I could feel myself passing out. When I woke up, there were men standing over me with guns. They thought—I had done it."

Daly paused. "There was no trace of the Comanches."

"Satisfied, Mr. Chuka?" Valois asked. "Ever hear of Comanches doing a thing like that?"

Chuka ignored Valois. "What do you think happened, Lieutenant?" He asked.

"The Comanches always take their own dead," Daly said, "if they can. I don't know why they didn't kill me—or for that matter, why they didn't take the woman's scalp. There was no sign of their having been there. No sign."

"Horses leave prints," Valois said.

"The only thing I can figure is that the prints were kicked over by the other horses. There must have been a hundred troops and civilians there when I woke up."

Valois looked at Chuka. "Well?"

Chuka looked at Daly. "It could be true," he said slowly. "And then again it could be a lie."

Daly looked up at Chuka. "It is the truth. Before God in heaven, it is the truth."

"Well," Chuka observed, tilting his head to one side, "you sure musta convinced a lot of people; otherwise you wouldn't be here, but hung and buried."

Chuka looked at Valois. "You agree, Colonel?"

Valois did not reply. In the moment of silence that followed there was the quick opening and closing of the door. The Sheppards were gone.

Valois spun around and looked at his officers. "Good night, gentlemen," he said easily.

The room was cleared, leaving only Chuka and Valois. Chuka moved, finally, stretching and stepping to the door.

He paused and looked down at Valois seated before the table, staring at his half-filled glass of whiskey. "Did he do it, Colonel?" Chuka asked.

Colonel Stuart Valois turned and looked at Chuka. He stood, buttoned his tunic and stepped to the door. Both men stood in the darkness of the gallery.

"He did it," Valois said.

"But—"

"He killed the husband and the hired hand and raped the woman. The Indians attacked after it was all over with." Valois took a deep breath.

"Then the Indian tracks were wiped out by the others."

"Yes, but can you see twelve Comanches letting an officer sit outside a house taking pot shots at them while they rape the woman? Then sneak off? And lose the chance to take the hair of everybody in sight?"

"Then why wasn't he hung?" Chuka asked.

"There were eight officers on the court-martial, and every one of them had fought and suffered at the hands of the Comanches, and until that time, Daly had been a good soldier. His story was weak, but there was no real reason not to believe him. The prosecution had very little. He was acquitted and returned to duty."

"When you caught up with the Indians, you learned the truth."

"The truth. By that time it was too late. It would do little good to open it up again. He denied it and refused to resign. He was sent here, to Clendennon."

"To you."

"To me, Mr. Chuka."

"You're pretty good. You know how to draw blood from a man," Chuka said.

"Daly, and a few others, Mr. Chuka, will either rot here, desert or be killed. This is the end for them. The others—" Valois shrugged, "They may yet be soldiers."

"And that's your job," Chuka said, "Making them over."

"Not job, Mr. Chuka. Orders. A soldier never has a job, only orders."

Valois drew himself up. "Good night, Mr. Chuka."

"Good night, Colonel," Chuka said easily. Valois took several steps away when Chuka spoke. "Oh, Colonel—!"

"Yes?"

"Mind if I ask you a question?"

"Not at all, Mr. Chuka."

"How old are you?"

Colonel Stuart Valois hesitated only a moment. "I'll be twenty-five on the twenty-first of November."

Chuka nodded, politely.

"Now may I ask you a question?" Valois asked.

Chuka nodded again.

"How many men have you killed?"

Chuka was slow in answering. It was something often asked and seldom answered. It was not something he was proud of. Valois stood waiting. "I lost count, Colonel," Chuka said. "But it was sixteen the last time I took notice."

"Were they fair fights?"

"That's another question," Chuka said evenly.

"You needn't reply." Valois started to turn away.

"Fifteen were fair," Chuka said.

"Fair?"

"They were facing me. They had a chance."

"And the sixteenth?" Valois asked.

"I killed him down on the Traces. I shot him in the back of the head. But that was after he stuck a knife in me and tried to steal my horse."

"Then," Valois said gently, "he had a chance also. Didn't he?"

"You might say so, Colonel."

"Good night, Chuka," Valois said.

"Good night, Colonel," Chuka replied.

Colonel Stuart Valois walked along the gallery toward his quarters at the far side of the Fort. Automatically his eyes searched for the sentinel on the wall and his ears sought the sound of the measured step. At the entrance to his quarters, he stopped a moment and leaned against the door, shivering slightly. He looked out across the parade grounds. Clendennon was quiet. He wondered if it would remain so. Somewhere out beyond the walls, a man, Lou Trent, was doing a job. Depending on the way Trent did his job might well answer the question of whether the quiet of Clendennon would be broken. His thoughts wandered—somewhere in the back of his mind words came echoing down to him from the halls of West Point—"For the want of a nail the shoe is lost, for want of a shoe the horse is lost, for want of a horse the rider is lost." For the want of a rider, the message was lost, for the want of a message, the battle was lost—All for the want of a nail—

Stuart Valois shrugged, shivered once more and eased into his quarters. The room was warm. Hahnsbach would have been the one to see that his fire was going. There was a small light—Hahnsbach again.

It was a small room, a desk, two chairs, bed, gun rack, map file. The spare, bare essentials of the military man, of the commander who would have little time to spend in leisure. Valois' hand touched the leather bindings on a half-dozen books his mother had sent to him and that he had not yet been able to read. He picked them up one by one and read the titles. Stendhal, *The Red and the Black*; Boswell, *Life of Samuel Johnson*—

He stood perfectly still in the center of the room and stared. He saw nothing in the room. He was seeing something out of the past, even beyond when he was a cadet at the Point.

Maryland. The isolated eastern shore and the broad sweep of the Atlantic Ocean from the Virginia to the Delaware line, and a boy and a girl riding along the beaches. Stuart Valois and his younger sister, Roberta, fleeing before the wind on their mounts, laughing, racing.

Valois, the boy, had never wanted to be anything but a soldier. He had often wondered, in later years, when recalling the day he announced firmly to his father, "I shall become a soldier, Father," why this decision had been made, what had been the turning point in his life.

There was no military history in the Valois family. Not for a hundred and fifty years. Planters, horsemen, and a grandfather successful in shipping, but no soldiers, except way back when there were three Valois' with Washington at Valley Forge.

He did remember that as a child someone had visited the house and given him lead soldiers. Six magnificent French cavaliers mounted on fine horses. Could such a small thing as this have taken him from the family tradition of squire life, planting, the life of a merchant?

No matter now. It had happened. From his earliest recollections, he had read everything he could lay his hands on regarding the life of a soldier. And when the war of rebellion had started, three different times, the youth, Valois, had run away to join the Blue, only to be sent back each time. He followed the war as closely as a military strategist and correctly predicted the outcome a year before Lee's surrender.

There was no difficulty in getting Stuart Valois into West Point, from which he had graduated with honors, and where he had met Kathleen Robby—

Suddenly Colonel Stuart Valois was shaken out of his deep memory with the image of Kathleen's face before him.

And as he had done since the day she died, a month before their wedding day, Valois clenched his teeth and forced himself to return to the present.

There were serious problems to consider, should Trent return with bad news. He tried to focus on his command, the troops of Clendennon; but thoughts of them only served to invoke the memory again.

The question of whether he could depend upon his troops only served to bring to mind why Stuart Valois was in this situation to begin with. Upon Kathleen's death, Stuart Valois had turned to bitter, driving perfection as a soldier. He devoted every waking moment to research and understanding his studies in the art and the balances of war, the reasons for the winner, winning, and the reasons for the loser, losing.

In a time when the country was sick of war, when everywhere one looked, from one end of the land to the other, there was evidence of the bitter conflict, in such times, Stuart Valois' inner drive and intensity to wipe out the memory of Kathleen Robby served him in his profession. Again and again he was given difficult commands, and each time Stuart Valois came through successfully. And with each success, came a promotion. Until finally, he had been made Lieutenant-Colonel and given Clendennon.

He began to remove his boots, slowly, still thoughtful, when he realized that it was the face of Evangeline Sheppard that had set him to thinking about Kathleen. He paused, boot in hand, and stared at the light. They were much alike in their faces, and curiously, though Mrs. Sheppard was obviously a whore, alike in manner as well.

He stretched out on the bunk and considered the troops at Clendennon, one at a time, summoning up each man's face and record, side by side in his mind's eye. One man at a time, through his entire command, Valois examined the man and his past record, his behavior since arriving at Clendennon, trying to determine if the man could be depended upon should Hanu strike.

It was an exhausting hour. It proved futile. Valois did not think there was more than a half dozen that were worth his trust. He was nearly convinced, on the basis of their records, their behavior and their proven inferiority as soldiers, that all but a few would desert.

He sat up and reached for one of the books beside his bed. He did not look at the title. Opening the book at random, he began to read aloud, forcing himself to study each word, one at a time, grasp its meaning, then another word, then another and another —

Outside the carefully measured step of the sentry on the wall counted cadence through the cold and silent night.

Chapter Three

EARLIER that evening, some time before the informal gathering in the officers' mess had been switched from a friendly atmosphere to one of tension, Señorita Helena Chavez stood before the window in her room and studied the silent and ghostly figures of the watch etched against the moonlit sky. The towers, the spiked tops of the logs on the outer wall, the sentinels themselves, all silhouettes. The parade grounds were empty. No lights shone except those in the officers' mess. Behind her, Helena could hear the rustle of silken petticoats as Veronica Klietz prepared for bed. Helena herself had not moved to undress. She still wore her mantilla and comb, her gloves and carried her fan.

"Come to bed, Helena," Veronica said. "What do you see in the night that interests you so?"

Helena did not reply.

The rustling of the petticoats stopped. There was a long, deep silence in the room when the laughter from the officers' mess could be heard, the voices carrying through the dark, cold night clearly and distinctively.

"Make up your mind to it, Helena," Veronica Klietz said. "It has been arranged. It must be so."

"It has been arranged," Helena said, turning from the window, dropping her fan to the bed. "But I have not yet made up my mind to it."

"That will come, child," Veronica said. "The daughter of Augustino Chavez has given her word."

"No. My father gave his word. I had nothing to do with it," Helena said, a faint trace of sadness creeping into her voice.

"But you will do nothing to pervert your father's wishes?" Veronica asked, her voice sharpening.

"I will do nothing."

Veronica Klietz sat down on the bed and studied her charge. Veronica was still a handsome woman at fifty. Her hair was as black as night and her eyes were as gray as the morning frost. Mechanically she began to take down her hair, and then slowly, without notice, following a lifetime of habit, began to make two long plaits of her hair. "A marriage like this one, Helena, will do many things for you."

"I know."

"We have been over it—"

"We have, Veronica."

"But you have not made up your mind to it?"

"No."

"Listen, child," Veronica Klietz said, "what do you know of life? How can you know anything when you have been protected by your father and brothers—and before that, the Sisters of the Holy Name in Vera Cruz? Do you think yourself capable of making a decision of this nature? A marriage is an eternity. It is endless. And the deepest feelings have nothing whatsoever to do with life."

"You have told me. Papa has told me," Helena said, pulling hard at one finger of her glove. The sadness in her voice of a moment before was gone. Her tone was sharp, biting.

"A man is a man—"

"No."

"—but the difference between them does not lie in their face, or the touch of their hands—"

"It does," Helena Chavez said sharply.

"Helena!" Veronica Klietz said quickly. "I will not have you speak to me in that tone of voice."

Helena turned away and faced the window again.

"A man who will protect you, provide for you, raise your children in the true faith—a man with the grace and ease of a gentleman, a man with whom you can live from day to day, week to week, year to year, in comfort—this is important. Nothing else matters."

"How would you know?" Helena's voice cut through the darkened room like a knife.

"*Helena*! Apologize at once!"

Helena sighed and remained silent. Neither of them spoke until Veronica was finished with her hair.

"I am sorry," Helena said, her voice softer, but with none of the bitterness of her earlier tone lessened.

The older woman stood and walked to Helena, began to undo the dark folds of hair. Her hands were gentle, loving.

"I know what is in your mind," Veronica said, with tenderness creeping into her voice. "You are thinking of those moments when—you are taken."

Helena stiffened.

"Hush," Veronica said. "I am an old woman and I am wise. If this were not so, your father, Augustino, would not have asked me to see to the arrangements in New York with the family of Don Miguel."

A shudder passed through Helena Chavez' body at the sound of the name.

"Yes, that is what is in your mind," Veronica said. "You are thinking of those moments when you will be alone with your husband. Yet it is all in your hands, and your hands alone, to make the difference between that act of love becoming one of joy—or of pain."

"Yes!" Helena said, spinning around. "Those are my thoughts, Señora. A stranger in my bed. His hands on me, his uninvited kisses on my lips! Yes! Yes! These are my thoughts—" The outburst was left hanging, there was no end as Veronica's soothing hands went quickly to Helena's cheeks, holding them between her palms.

"A man will proceed. He will not stop. He will not go away. He will not leave you alone. And he will not tire of you. It will happen again and again and again. And it is up to you, Helena Chavez, to make the difference—if it is to be joy—or pain and sadness."

"This talk is disgusting, Señora," Helena said bitterly.

"As a child, I spent some time on my uncle's rancho in Durango. My uncle would ride through the grass and point to the animals—this one—that one—and that one. These were taken back to the enclosure behind the stables where the bull waited—"

She strode across the room. "And now, Señora, someone has pointed his whip at me, and I am being escorted to New York—where the bull is waiting!"

Veronica Klietz brought up her arm and slapped the younger woman a stinging blow across the face. "Go to bed. We will not talk of this anymore. You are a disgraceful young woman. I have tried to be patient with you and explain—"

"Yes, explain," Helena said. "What? That I am to be bartered off by my loving father and willing brothers, so that the fortunes of Don Miguel can be brought into the household of Augustino Chavez!

Señora, tell me the difference between myself and the animals my uncle pointed out to be brought to the bull?"

"More of this, Helena, and I will return you to your father."

"My father? So that I may be returned to the Sisters of the Holy Name in Vera Cruz, exiled from life because I refuse to be used as a trade?"

"I will not allow you to speak of your loving father in this manner, Señorita."

"Loving father! If he loves me, why does he permit—no, not permit, but insist on selling me into slavery?"

"Enough!" Veronica Klietz shrilled. "We will remain here at Fort Clendennon until the stage returns from Granada—and take us back to Trinidad. I will send word to your father in the morning."

"So, Señora," Helena said bitterly, "the destiny of Helena Chavez has been sealed. Her fate, determined. She is to be placed in a stone castle and told to repent for the rest of her life because she refused to be subjected to—the bull!"

"I am glad, Señorita," Veronica Klietz said in a cold and chilling tone, "to have discovered your true character before going any further. At least your father and family will be spared the disgrace of your conduct in public. God be merciful on you in the years ahead when you relive this moment."

"That is a presumption, Señora," Helena said. "I may well look back upon this moment as my hour of deliverance—from the bulls!"

"You irreverent creature! No more!" Veronica Klietz screamed. She crossed herself and whispered a prayer.

"Why the bitterness, Señora?" Helena asked. "Is it perhaps that you were sold into slavery yourself? Perhaps when the stranger crept into your bed—"

Veronica Klietz retreated into her last defense. She dropped to her knees, unmindful of the bare, cold floor and began to pray. Her eyes closed, her head bowed, her lips moving in the incantation, she fought off the words and the evocation of Helena's accusation, seeking refuge from blasphemy.

Veronica Klietz prayed steadily for an hour, long after Helena had undressed and slipped into bed.

Helena did not sleep. She watched the light of the moon as it traveled across the sky, moving the shadows in the room, and wept silently.

The irrevocable had finally happened. There was no way to undo what had been done. She did not weep for this, but for the memory of her father. Her papa, who had always come to her room, regardless of how late it was, and kissed her good night, his face smelling as often of sweat and grime from his long work on the ranch as from cologne when he returned from a ball.

She turned over on her side as Veronica slipped silently into bed and cried for hours, reliving past days when she was the princess of the world and there was only the future to look forward to, when she would live happily ever after.

Helena did not know what time it was when she heard the gates opening. She went to the window, saw a rider move through the one-horse gate and then saw the figure of a man emerge from the shadows, coming from the direction of the stables. The man stepped into the moonlight and she saw it was the pistolero—Chuka. Then, suddenly overwhelmingly tired and chilled from standing in the cold room, dressed in nothing but her nightgown, she slipped back into bed.

Her last thought before falling into a deep, exhaustive sleep was the look on the Mother Superiors' face when she appeared at the gates of the Sisters of The Holy Name in Vera Cruz.

Veronica Klietz did not move. She lay perfectly still and listened to the silent weeping of Helena Chavez and wept herself, seeing from the height of her maturity and wisdom the course her charge now would follow. It would be a simple and direct course, with little or no change in the ritual. Return home, and once there, watch as Helena was subjected to the temper and fury of her father, her brothers, the relatives. It would last a week—ten days, perhaps—then word would come from New York: Where is Helena?

Another week of her family's temper, and finally fury would change into pleas. Love would take over in the hearts of Augustino and the brothers. They would say to themselves that Helena was younger than they thought, not as wise or mature as they had believed and did not quite understand what the marriage to Don Miguel would mean. Patiently, each in turn would attempt to persuade Helena and try to make her understand.

Through it all, Helena would say nothing. Another message would come from New York, from Don Miguel. This time it would have to be answered.

Then, one last attempt would be made by the family to show Helena the error of her ways, and when she rejected their final plea, she would be dismissed.

The padre would take over then. He would be the last. If he could not talk sense to her, if he could not get her to change her mind, then all would be lost. In the meantime, while this last recourse was being run, with the patient old priest doing his best to get Helena to change her mind—and in so doing, have Augustino Chavez indebted to him, which could be turned into a healthy contribution to the church—the family would ignore her. She would be, as Augustino Chavez would have told her, dead to them.

But the old priest would fail. Veronica Klietz knew this.

The final pleas would be made, and Helena would not recant. Preparations would be made for her transport and entrance into the convent.

And it was for all of this that Veronica Klietz was weeping.

She did not sleep until Helena Chavez' quivering stopped, until the last sigh was gone. Then in the silence of the room, she slipped out of bed and, on her knees, prayed for some solution.

Once more in bed, Veronica Klietz closed her eyes, comforted by her faith and belief that whatever came to pass was of Divine will. She had made her supplication. An earnest and devout heart had been placed on the altar. There was nothing more for her to do. Whatever happened from this moment on, Veronica Klietz believed, would be because it had been willed to be so.

She slept.

Chapter Four

ON the morning of November 17th, reveille at Fort Clendennon was no different from any other morning. The bugle was blown at five-thirty A.M. The officers and other men had one-half hour to prepare for a full inspection by Valois. This included all officers, their quarters, all troops and their quarters, as well as the entire area within the walls of the Fort. No one was ever excused from this inspection at Clendennon, unless permission was granted personally by Valois.

Chuka, aroused by the bugle, moved to the window of the officers' mess where he had bedded down before the stove and stared sleepily at the scene. Though still quite dark, a full half-hour before sunup, there was enough gray in the sky for a clear view of the parade grounds. At five to six, last call was bugled and the men, carrying full equipment, began to pour out of their quarters and fall in. Three squads of ten men each, with the commander from each squad, Lieutenants Daly and Mack and Captain Carrol, moving through the ranks checking on the men. Major Cook stood ahead of the others, while Sergeant Hahnsbach, although technically in formation, stood to one side with the muster sheet.

At precisely six A.M., Colonel Stuart Valois emerged from his quarters, received Major Cook's salute and looked at his men. "Carry on, Major Cook," Valois said.

"Sergeant!" Major Cook barked.

Hahnsbach took one step forward, turned and faced the three squads. "Flag dee-taaaaal!" Hahnsbach thundered.

Four men took one step forward, moving with military precision, formed into ranks of two abreast and stood perfectly still while waiting for the order.

"Flag dee-taaaaal! Marrch!" Hahnsbach roared.

The men stepped off as one and executed perfect military cadence to the flagpole, stopped, broke ranks and hooked the corners of the flag to the halyard. The ascent of the flag was brisk, one flowing upward movement. The moment the flag moved upward, the bugle sounded and continued until the flag was close-hauled and tied down. The detail of four men fell into rank again and returned to their positions.

"Major," Valois said once more.

"Sergeant!" Major Cook said.

In a big booming voice, Sergeant Otto Hahnsbach began to call the muster.

"Major Cook!"

"Ho!"

"Captain Carrol!"

"Ho!"

"Lieutenant Daly!"

"Ho!"

"Lieutenant Mack!"

"Ho!"

"Corporal Dreen!"

"Ho!"

The barrel-chested voice of sergeant Hahnsbach continued through to the end. When the last name was called, Sergeant Hahnsbach turned to Major Cook. "Louis Trent, Army scout, is on a mission sir, and has not returned to the Fort," Hahnsbach snapped a stiff salute and stood at attention.

Major Cook repeated word for word what the Sergeant had said, ending up by saluting Colonel Valois.

"I want to be informed the minute the scout returns to the post, Major Cook."

"Yes, Sir."

"All right, Major Cook."

Cook took three steps forward and fell in beside Valois. Both men stepped off together and began their inspection rounds of the Fort. The formation of men remained at attention.

Chuka shook his head and turned back to the stove, sat down and began to pull on his boots. He was dressed and seated at the table, very carefully cleaning his carbine and six-gun, the parts on the table, a chamois is his hand, going over each piece with patience and care, when the door opened and Valois, followed by Cook, entered the room.

"Good morning, Mr. Chuka," Valois said.

"Morning, Colonel."

"I hope you slept well."

"I slept well, as long as I could. You get up mighty early around here."

"Five-thirty is not an uncivilized hour, Mr. Chuka," Valois answered.

"No, but four A.M. is, Colonel."

"Four?"

"That's when the mess detail came in here to clean up after your party last night."

Valois smiled. "Do you always take such good care of your weapon, Sir?"

"Colonel, this gun saved my life sixteen times. I'm beholden to it. I keep it clean."

"For seventeen?"

"Sometimes they come two at a time. May be seventeen and eighteen," Chuka said dryly.

"Good morning," Valois said. He turned and left the room. Major Cook hesitated a moment, looked at Chuka, started to speak, then hurried after Valois.

By the time the sun had broken over the eastern flats, Fort Clendennon was moving through the cold morning in pursuit of its daily routine. After finishing with his guns, Chuka went from the mess to the cook house where three men bustled and sweated before a huge stove, preparing breakfast. Chuka leaned in on the half-door. "Any chance of getting a little hot water for a shave?"

One of the men turned around, smiled a toothless welcome and waved Chuka in. "Help yourself."

"Thank you."

Chuka moved into the steamy, warm, good-smelling kitchen. "That coffee smells fine."

"There's a mug," the man said. "You got your razor with you?"

"Yeah."

"You can shave in here if you want to. We're going to be shoveling grub into the officers' mess soon."

"That's all right," Chuka said and moved out of their way as they worked, sipping the coffee and loosening his shirt. "Why all the spit and polish out there with the flag raising?"

"Oh, you mean the inspection," the man replied. "Every morning."

"But why?"

"Military discipline, as the way he puts it."

"The Colonel?"

"Clendennon is like a jail, Mister; only it ain't. We're too good to throw out of the Army, and we ain't quite bad enough to be shot or hung—and at the same time, too bad to soldier with anybody but our own kind. So we pull Clendennon."

Chuka shrugged and continued shaving. As the kitchen crew began to load food onto trays for removal to the officers' mess, Henry and Jake, followed by the stage driver and the gun guard entered the kitchen.

"Coffee smells mighty good!" Henry said. He noticed Chuka standing in the rear of the room. "Morning."

Jake nodded. Baldwin, the driver, and Howard, the gun guard, greeted everyone in the kitchen with a general wave of their hands and then all of them were swept back out of the way by the busy cooks. Henry grabbed four mugs and filled them with coffee, then he and Jake retired to Chuka's side as the troopers began to line up at the door of the kitchen.

"Think we're going to get snow between here and Cheyenne?" Chuka asked Baldwin.

The driver shook his head. "Snow would be about right for this time of the year. And it's cold enough. But we ain't going nowheres until that scout comes back."

Chuka paused. "Yeah?"

"Just got the word from the Colonel," Howard said.

"Stage is staying right here until we get some word or other—"

"Hanu?"

"Hanu," Baldwin affirmed with a nod of his head.

"There's been some kind of a build-up of ragged-tailed bands of all kinds of Indians sticking around Hanu's camp."

"That's nothing unusual," Chuka said. "It's happening everywhere."

"Up to Montana country for sure," Henry said. Baldwin shook his head. "That's true, but this time there's a difference. Hanu is supposed to be moving down off Rush Creek for his winter lodges at the Red River watershed soon. When you got four or five hundred braves on the prod, that's a difference."

"*Four or five hundred!*" Chuka was amazed.

"That's the report the scout has been bringin' in," Baldwin said. "Damn that old buzzard, Hanu!" Baldwin said suddenly. "Don't he know he can't *do* nothing!"

"Nothing lasting, anyways," Howard added dourly.

Chuka finished shaving his neck. "Well, don't go cussing him out yet. He ain't done nothing," he grinned, "yet."

Baldwin stood. "That *yet* is what's got my short hair half rose already. But I still got to make time. If I don't get back to Trinidad in a puffin' hurry, I might get caught in the snow. And Danny Boy Howard here has a woman expecting a baby in about two weeks."

Baldwin put the empty mug down. "Come'n, Dan. We can be ready to roll if we get the word. We'll hitch the teams."

The driver and the gun guard pushed their way through the front door where Clendennon troopers were lining up for their breakfast.

"How about us, Chuka?" Henry asked. "If there's a prod of four or five hundred Injuns, we might jest as well wait for the scout too."

Chuka thought a moment, then nodded. "No use asking for it," he agreed.

The three men left the kitchen soon afterward and walked across the parade grounds toward the officers' mess. They stepped inside, removed their hats and sat down at a table.

"Did you hear that the stage can't leave yet, Mr. Chuka?" John Sheppard asked the moment the big man sat down.

"I heard," Chuka said. He then turned and spoke to Helena Chavez. "Morning, Miss Chavez. Hope you had a good sleep."

"Yes, thank you," Helena said, her eyes downcast.

Veronica Klietz sat beside her, stiff-backed, eyes bright and hard. She did not reply, nor did she look at Chuka as he leaned on the table and looked past Helena and spoke to her. "Morning."

Chuka shrugged and looked up to see Henry watching him. The leathery-faced man shrugged and winked. Chuka winked back and turned to look at Evangeline. He smiled. "How are you feeling, Eve?" He asked, easily, friendly.

She raised her eyes and gave him a tired smile. "That whiskey we used to drink back at the Casino in Trinidad was spring water compared to the Colonel's stock." She looked over at Valois. He grinned and nodded, bowed his head in a gracious way.

Eve turned back to Chuka. "I feel terrible. I'm not used to that government liquor."

The men at the table chuckled sympathetically, even Helena managed a smile; but Veronica Klietz stared straight ahead in silence.

"I *don't* see," Sheppard was saying to Colonel Valois, "why the stage line shouldn't take responsibility for this. They should have warned all the passengers that there was an Indian threat—before we left Trinidad."

"You haven't been scalped yet, Johnny," Eve said.

"I'm not thinking just about myself, but the lives of three women," Sheppard said, "Señora Klietz, Señorita Chavez and, of course you, my dear."

Veronica Klietz put down her cup of coffee and looked At Valois. "I do not wish to burden you further, Colonel; but if it is possible, Señorita Chavez and myself would like to remain here at Fort Clendennon until the stage returns from Granada. We will not be completing our journey, but are returning to Mexico."

"Noblesse oblige, Señora Klietz. But I assure you there is very little to be alarmed over. Talk and rumor is one thing, but attacking an armed fort—that is quite another. If necessary, to relieve all of your minds," Valois said, "I will detail an escort to accompany the stage on to Granada, as soon as the scout returns."

"Well, now, that's more like it," Sheppard said.

"I'm afraid I did not make myself quite clear, Colonel Valois," Señora Klietz continued. "Under no circumstances will Señorita Chavez and myself go on to Granada—unless, of course, it is not permitted to remain here at Fort Clendennon until the coach returns."

Chuka saw the knuckles of Helena's hands turn white. She stifled a gasp.

"But Señora, if it is the Indian threat—"

"It has nothing whatsoever to do with Indians, Colonel Valois. It is a personal matter."

"Then, Señora, let me offer you the hospitality of Fort Clendennon for as long as you wish to stay."

"Thank you," Veronica Klietz said. "Your consideration and kindliness will not go unnoticed in circles of importance, Colonel Valois."

Valois waved away the remarks. "Please, ladies and gentlemen, stay as long as you wish, and anything you desire, please tell Major Cook and he will see to it. I must return to duty." Valois stood and walked to the door. Mack, Daly and Carrol stood and followed him from the room.

"I hope there isn't anything serious, Miss Chavez," Chuka said quietly. "If there is anything I can do—"

She looked at him briefly. "There is nothing you can do, Señor Chuka. Thank you."

"I hardly think there would be anything you could do, for a lady, Chuka," Major Cook said.

Chuka looked up and studied Major Cook in a sidelong glance. "Oh, I don't know," he said quietly. "Never can tell when you might step into a nest of rattlers in this part of the country."

"Or sit down to eat with a skunk," Major Cook added.

Chuka's voice became hard. "What are you trying to do, man?"

The harsh question hung heavily in the air. Major Cook chose to ignore it. He stood, avoiding Chuka, and looked at Helena and Veronica. "Ladies, to pass the time, I would be delighted to show you what there is to see of Fort Clendennon."

"Yes, yes, that would be an excellent idea," Sheppard said. "Come, Eve, we will all stroll. The cold air will make you feel better."

"I'd rather stay here, Johnny, if you don't mind. I need some more of this coffee." She gave her husband an affectionate smile. "I'll talk to Chuka if he doesn't have anything more important to do."

"Just take care of my horse, and I'd much rather talk to you," Chuka said.

Sheppard walked around the table and kissed his wife on the cheek. "All right, Eve. You did get pretty soused last night".

Señora Klietz and Helena Chavez stood up and walked to the door. They were halfway across the room when Chuka stooped down and picked up a lace glove. He stepped forward and held it out to Helena. "You dropped this, Señorita."

Major Cook held out his hand, and Chuka immediately withdrew the glove. "I don't think it would fit you, Major."

"Thank you." Helena quickly held out her hand.

"A pleasure, ma'am," Chuka said and dropped the glove into her palm. For a split second their eyes met and held.

"Helena!" Veronica Klietz's voice was sharp and insistent.

Chuka stood at the door and watched them walk away. Henry and Jake eased up to his side and then through the door. "We'll take care of your pony," Henry said.

He and Jake turned and made a courtly gesture to Eve. "Good morning, Mrs. Sheppard," Henry said and then both men left.

After a long while, Chuka turned back to the table and sat at the far end. He poured himself another cup of coffee. He looked at Eve. "How come you up and married Sheppard, Eve? You looked like you were pretty well set, back there in Trinidad."

"Set—or stuck?"

"Well—"Chuka said.

She sighed. "It was the only way I could get out of that hole."

"Good enough. But there must have been—easier ways."

"Don't laugh at me, Chuka. Johnny is a man, the first one in a long time that asked me to marry him." Her eyes closed and she leaned back into her chair and wiped her forehead. "I'm going to start sweatin' in a minute. Always did on the morning after."

"Want me to hold your head?"

"I won't get sick. I just feel like it, but I never do."

"How long were you in Trinidad?" Chuka asked.

"Too long. Nearly two years. Long enough to learn about Holly and his ways."

"Yeah, old Holly sure had an iron grip on that part of the country."

44

Eve's hands came down hard on the table. She stared at Chuka, who was not looking at her. "You said had—"

"Did I?"

"Wait a minute—" Eve said. "Two weeks ago, out in the dry country, there was talk about something going on. Then you drifted into town."

"How's your head?" Chuka asked.

"You hired out to the Salvatore group, the small ranchers who were fighting Holly—"

"I was taken on as a hand at Sal's place," Chuka said.

"You said Holly *had*, meaning he doesn't now. Is he dead?"

Chuka did not reply.

"Is he, Chuka?"

"Leave it alone, Eve," Chuka said evenly.

"That means you had to get past Dory and Akins to get to Holly."

"Leave it alone, Eve." Chuka's voice came out hard and flat.

Evangeline Sheppard smiled, but her teeth were clenched. "Damn you, Mark Holly. May your soul rot in hellfire through all time!"

"You hated him that much?"

"I hated him that much. In case it occurred to you, which I'm sure it hasn't, ever wonder how I got to a hole in the mountains like Trinidad? Well, I'll tell you. It was Mark Holly. I met him when he was on a buying trip, up in Cheyenne. We were going to be married when we got to Trinidad, only when we got to Trinidad, I found out he was already married. I took a shotgun and went after him. He caught me, beat me nearly to death."

Chuka let out a long, low whistle. "I didn't know he was that kind—"

"Well, he was. Didn't Salvatore and the other tell you?"

"They told me things, but nothing like this. You must have kept it to yourself."

"It was either keep it to myself, or get beaten up again."

She looked at Chuka. Her eyes began to swim. But she had not told Chuka everything. No, not everything.

She had not told him that she loved Mark Holly.

Evangeline Sheppard did not spell out in detail the emotions she had known in Cheyenne, nor would it have been possible if she wanted to.

Markson Holly. All of him and everything about him, the cruelty in his smile that was also a smile of life, the swagger to his shoulders, the sure way he had with himself and—and—so much more.

No, she had not told Chuka what those hours and few days in Cheyenne had meant to a woman like Evangeline. There was a lifetime, an eternity, in the time between meeting and loving Mark Holly for the first time and when he had beaten her. But even the fact of his marriage had had little effect on her feelings. The beating had only a little more.

It had taken months of waiting, hoping he would come to Trinidad and say it was over with his wife and that Eve—Eve would be the one for him.

Yes, she thought, she kept it to herself. But not because she was afraid of another beating. But rather she accepted the beating and kept alive her hope that Mark Holly would come back to her. If she told, it would be out in the open, and then he would never return.

So she hung on, took a job and hung on. When he did come to Trinidad on business, when he went to the Casino to play cards or get drunk, when he turned to her and wanted her to go to bed with him, Eve hung onto her hope that he would come to her one time and tell her he would stay.

How long had it gone on like that? Eight months—a year?

And in-between his visits, there was no one. She only saw much later that the others had not attempted to sleep with her because of Mark Holly, and only partially because she didn't look at anyone else. They were afraid of Mark Holly, not her.

Then his visits to Trinidad became more and more frequent, and his private visits to her more natural and easy.

No, Eve thought, not easy, taken-for-granted.

She remembered clearly how she rationalized this to herself. There was going to be no change in Mark Holly's status; he was not going to leave his wife and marry Evangeline. The relationship existed beyond this point because Eve wanted it to, because she was perfectly willing to have a little part of Mark Holly, rather than no part at all.

Then the awakening. The full realization of how she had deluded herself came quickly, surely, with finality. That September morning over a year ago.

Holly had not been in Trinidad for several weeks. The work preparing for the winter was taking all his time, and the fall roundup of cattle, to be taken on north to Wyoming grass, was in full swing. Then that man showed up.

Gregson—a cattle buyer from Cheyenne, down to look over Holly's herd. It had been a hard summer and the herd was low. Getting them to Wyoming grass was a matter of saving everything Mark Holly had, and there was Gregson, with ready cash, to buy futures on the herd. Holly had come to town that morning to meet Gregson, and there was some reluctance on Gregson's part to hand over hard cash on the future of cattle that looked as scraggly as Mark Holly's herd. Holly was desperate. They had been drinking most of the morning, and at eleven, as Eve was just getting up, they appeared at her door.

Red-faced, half-drunk, both of them pushed into her room.

"Didn't I tell you she was a pretty?" Holly had said to Gregson. And while Gregson leered at her, Holly spoke in her ear. "Treat him nice, eh, Eve?"

Then Holly was out the door and Gregson was behind her, giggling, pawing her, his hands ripping her clothing.

Eve fought. She struggled and bit and scratched and then, suddenly, there was the hard thick fist exploding in her face, and it was all over.

From that moment on Eve began to hate—hate—hate—HATE—

"Eve!"

Evangeline Sheppard resisted the powerful hands on her shoulders.

"Eve!" Chuka was shaking her. "What's the matter with you'!"

She looked up; her eyes cleared. She jerked away, stepped back and looked at Chuka. Slowly, recognition came over her face as she remembered.

"Oh," she said, out of breath. Evangeline sank into the chair, exhausted. "He's dead?"

"Who?"

She could hardly speak. "Mark—Mark Holly—Is he dead?"

"Eve—leave it alone," Chuka said gently.

She looked up into his face. "Is—he—he—dead? Dammit! Answer me!"

"He's dead," Chuka said.

She slumped back to the table. "Dead—*dead!*"

Chuka poured her a drink, nearly a brimful of whiskey, and put it before her. "Drink it," Chuka said.

Eve took the glass, her hands shaking. Chuka had to help her. She swallowed with difficulty, some of the whiskey slopping onto her dress. She ignored it and gasped.

Chuka sat down and watched her. After a long time, she spoke, her voice firm and under control. "I owe you something, Chuka."

"You don't owe me, Eve."

"I owe you."

"No—"

"I owe you!" She said through her teeth.

"Look," he said softly, "whatever there was between you and Holly, you'd better forget it. He's dead—and you're alive."

She didn't respond.

"You hear me?" Chuka said. "If he hurt you bad, he paid for it."

"Paid? Do you think a quick bullet from a six-gun, a quick death, will make up for what he did to me?" She paused. "And not only to me. What about his wife? What the hell did she go through, knowing I was in town, and that he was coming in to see me? What about her hurt? And Salvatore and the small ranchers? A quick bullet from a gunfighter's gun can't make it up," she said bitterly. "But even so, I owe you."

"You don't owe me, Eve. And if it will make you feel easier, Mark Holly crawled."

Eve lifted her eyes. "You're just telling me that."

"I don't lie, Eve," Chuka said evenly.

"You're lying to me!"

"He *crawled*," Chuka said.

"Mark Holly would—" She stopped. "Whatever else he was, he wasn't a coward. I mean—"

Chuka set his teeth on edge. He stared her in the eye. "We caught him and some of his riders red-handed. They had burned down a house and two barns in one night."

"No, I don't want to know about it," Eve said suddenly.

Chuka pressed on. "We caught 'em. I called Holly out—me and him. He wouldn't come. He sent Dory and Akins. I got past both of them, and Holly tried to run for it. We caught him—"

Eve screamed, putting her hands over her ears. "NO!"

Chuka slumped back in his chair. He waited. She lowered her arms to the table, took the remains of the whiskey and drank it. After a moment, she nodded her head.

"We were going to bring him to Denver to stand trial. But then we learned that Salvatore's daughter, Maria, had been in the house. Salvatore had a Liverwright shotgun. Holly got down on his knees and begged Sal. He crawled on his knees and begged."

"He begged?" Eve asked, her voice firm.

"He *crawled* and *begged*," Chuka said. "Salvatore tore him in half with the Liverwright."

It was some time before Eve moved, or spoke. She stared at the empty glass. "I loved him, Chuka—"

"I figured as much."

"I'd—I'd like to be alone now, if you don't mind."

She stood up. "I think I'll get some of the clean, cold Colorado air."

Chuka nodded. Eve wiped her face, straightened her back and stepped to the door.

Outside, in the pale but welcome sunshine, the parade ground was a beehive of activity. Hammering sounds from the smithy rang through the crisp morning air. The good natured joking and laughing of the troops going through the morning routine of cleaning out the stables and caring for the horses could be heard now and then. Eve spotted Major Cook, Helena, Veronica and John Sheppard walking along the watch wall. Eve started after them, climbing to the catwalk.

"Johnny!" She called softly when she had come within a few feet of the group. Sheppard excused himself from the women and turned to his wife. "I want to talk to you a minute, Johnny."

Sheppard nodded. "All right. We can stroll in the opposite direction. My God, but the air is clear. You can see for miles."

"Johnny—"

"Yes?"

"There is something I want to tell you."

The tone of her voice made John Sheppard turn to look at her. "Eve, if this is a confession of some sort, don't. I—"

She cut him off, quickly, determinedly. "I've got something to say."

"Please—" Sheppard said, stopping and holding his wife's hands in his own. "I'm a grown man. I know what I'm doing."

"You don't. You didn't."

John Sheppard looked into his wife's eyes. He saw her turmoil in them and knew it would be impossible to stop her. "All right, Evangeline," he said gently, "if you feel you must tell me, go ahead."

It was difficult for Eve to begin, once she was free and sure that she wanted to talk. "You were just a ticket out of Trinidad to St. Louis, Johnny. I don't know if you remember it or not; but you never asked me to marry you. You were so drunk—" She paused and leaned against the piked logs. "You were so drunk, the preacher didn't want to marry us. In fact, you passed out."

"I gathered as much, Eve," Sheppard replied.

"Did you know Mark Holly?"

"Yes. Very well. I sold him a lot of equipment."

"Did you know I was—his—girl?"

"Yes. Everyone knew it."

"Did you know he was dead before you—asked me to drink with you that night, back in Trinidad?"

"No—is he?" Sheppard was a little surprised.

"He's dead." Eve said. "And you didn't know."

"I didn't know. Would it make any difference?"

"No—it adds."

"Adds to what, Eve?"

"I was going to get to St. Louis and skin you for as much as I could, Johnny, then leave you flat."

Sheppard scratched his chin. "I thought about that. But I had hoped—well, St. Louis is a long way away. I hoped to be able to change your mind—"

"Change my mind about what?"

"Leaving me," John Sheppard said, lowering his eyes. "I hoped I could change that—hard look around your eyes—when you looked at me—when I kissed you, as if you were holding back—"

Sheppard stopped and followed Eve's gaze out over the grasslands. "I knew about you and Holly. But I made up my mind last year—"

"Last year?"

"I saw you for the first time last year, Eve. I made up my mind in a small Ohio town—" He paused.

"I was in a hotel. Alone. Half-drunk, like any other night, to fight off being lonely, to help me go to sleep in an empty room—"

Eve was watching him closely.

"I remembered you and I made up my mind that if you were still in Trinidad when I came back, Mark Holly or not, I was going to—"

"To what, Johnny?" Evangeline asked.

"Ask you to marry me."

"You've thought about me—that long?" She asked.

"More than you will ever know, Eve."

Neither of them spoke for a long while. It was Eve who finally broke the silence between them. "Well, now we know."

"What?"

"If you can believe me, Johnny," Eve said, "I'll do my best—"

"Beautiful morning, isn't it?" John Sheppard said, turning to his wife and smiling.

Eve looked at him. Her eye traveled across the parade grounds and saw Chuka walking slowly toward the stables. "Yes," she said, "it is a beautiful morning."

John Sheppard took his wife by the arm and they continued their stroll around the catwalk, enjoying the warm morning sunshine.

Chapter Five

SARGEANT Hahnsbach had refused a direct commission three times in the course of his career. He was utterly and completely satisfied as an enlisted man. This decision to remain an enlisted man, resolved to absolute dedication to the Army, had never once been regretted by the big, tough Sergeant. Hahnsbach was the epitome of the soldier of his times, excellent horseman, crack shot, fearless, with unflinching loyalty to his commanding officer; the picture of the professional horse soldier.

In his years as an enlisted man, Hahnsbach had served with many good to excellent officers; but when he spotted your Lieutenant Valois, fresh from West Point, he recognized something of himself in the youthful officer. Hahnsbach had not known in the beginning, about Kathleen Robby, and the effect her death had on Stuart Valois; but he would not believe the squad gossip that Valois was just another brass plated Looey, eager for promotions and glory. Hahnsbach thought he recognized in Valois the same dedication to the Army that he himself felt and after working with the young man over a period of time, finally came to admire Stuart Valois as an officer or rare breed: accurate, just, open-minded, dedicated.

Again and again, Hahnsbach had seen Valois perform the impossible and never mention it. Once he was convinced that Valois' modesty was not false, he made it his business to work with and for Valois. It was not long before Hahnsbach's behind the scenes work with the enlisted men under Valois in the early commands became known to the young officer. It was not difficult to learn that Hahnsbach had been urging, threatening, bullying, even fighting, in some cases, for the whole hearted support of the troops serving under Valois. Yet when it became obvious to Valois that Hahnsbach was going out of his way to help him, he accepted it as that which was due to him from his sergeant. There was more to it than the military relationship of an officer to his sergeant. This was made known to Hahnsbach when, upon his first shift in commands, Valois exercised his rank by requesting that Hahnsbach be reassigned with him. Hahnsbach had expected it, and once this was done, the two men, a tough, burly sergeant and the young, purposeful officer became professionally inseparable. From post to post, command to command, Hahnsbach had followed Valois; and when Valois had taken Clendennon, Hahnsbach followed him to the frontier and took charge of the rebel soldiers with a sure hand. It only took two arguments and two fist fights to convince the troopers of Fort Clendennon that Sergeant Hahnsbach was not going to let them get away with a damn thing. Upon their arrival at Clendennon, Valois had explained the situation to Hahnsbach then gave him a free hand. With his usual confidence and control and grasp, Hahnsbach had started right in on the enlisted men and established his authority. Roughly, then, Clendennon was divided into two areas. Valois, the over-all commander, with special regard to the officers, and Hahnsbach in general command of the enlisted men.

Over the years, however, the two men had grown fond of each other beyond their military tasks, and though this fondness had never been expressed in any way, except through military exercises, Hahnsbach would look at Valois and think of the son he never had.

Sergeant Hahnsbach, then, was as apprehensive of the situation then existing at Clendennon and the threat of the explosion that might come, as Valois or Trent. There was no mistaking it, Hahnsbach thought grimly, as he watched a detail of soldiers working in the stables. It would be a miracle if Hanu did not strike. He cursed the stupidity of the brass at Forts Wallace and Garland for not recognizing the threat that was presented by nearly five hundred Indians on the move. "Hurry it up there!" He barked at a soldier, his voice yielding to his irritation.

"Aw, Sarge," the trooper complained.

"You want the latrine detail after this, Spivey?" Hahnsbach asked, his face glowering.

The man retreated under the blast. He had learned, as they all had, not to talk back or argue with Hahnsbach.

Hahnsbach turned from the stables and looked out over the parade ground, saw Major Cook and the stage passengers and then noticed the gunfighter walking toward him. With a practiced eye Hahnsbach took in every detail of the man. Hahnsbach, like most men on the frontier who lived simple, uncomplicated lives, disliked gunfighters. It was an instinctive dislike. A man with rattlesnake speed in his gun was not to be trusted.

Hahnsbach squared off before the wide doors of the stable and, arms akimbo, stuck out his jaw as Chuka approached. "The gunslick—" Hahnsbach said, his voice flat and even.

"The bucko Sergeant," Chuka said softly, sensing Hahnsbach's hostility toward him. He started to push past Hahnsbach and enter the stable, but the big Sergeant moved over and blocked his way. Chuka backed up. "My men are busy in there, gunslick. You'll have to wait." Hahnsbach folded his arms and stared at Chuka.

The movement in the stables lessened then stopped altogether. The men grew silent. The stable detail had felt the lash of Hahnsbach's tongue all morning and had been wondering where and when the big Sergeant's wrath would settle. But there wasn't one of them that didn't think Hahnsbach was asking for it by bracing the gunslick. Henry and Jake, who had been talking with Baldwin and Howard as the stagemen checked over the extensive leather trappings of the stagecoach rig, eased out the back of the stables. Neither Hahnsbach nor Chuka had moved.

Chuka looked beyond Hahnsbach to the interior of the stables. "Take a soldier, now, like those inside," he said amiably. "They have to do what they're told."

"But you do as you please, is that it, gunslick?" Hahnsbach said quickly.

"More or less."

"This time, gunslick, it's less. Turn your tail around and come back when we're finished."

"No," Chuka said slowly. "I'm going in now."

"If you draw that gun," Hahnsbach said, "I'll make you eat it."

"*If* I draw this gun, soldier, the only thing you'd eat from here on would be the wrong end of a daisy."

Hahnsbach grinned then laughed; a teasing chuckle that erupted as he stepped back a few paces and leaned on the edge of the stable door. "Caught you in a bind, didn't I gunslick? You see, there are too many witnesses to say you shot down an unarmed man." Hahnsbach's voice hardened. "So draw off, gunslick. You're tied up."

Chuka looked past Hahnsbach and saw the soldiers nudge each other in the ribs, their faces breaking into grins.

Chuka turned sideways, as if he intended to walk away, stopped and turned back. "Is this official? Are you acting as a soldier, telling me to stay out, or are you just pushing for fun?"

"I don't like gunslicks," Hahnsbach said. "Is that plain enough?"

"Oh!" Chuka said, nodding. Very slowly, he reached down and untied the holster from his leg and began to unbuckle his belt. He watched

Hahnsbach, seeing surprise suddenly appear in the big Sergeant's eyes, then noting that his surprise changed to anger. "Hey, Jake!"

"Yeah!" The tall, thin man moved toward Chuka. "Hold my weapon, will you?"

"Why sure—"

"And see to it I don't have to fight the whole Army."

Hahnsbach stepped forward, his jaw thrust out. "No one will bother you—but me, gunslick!"

Hahnsbach swung, without warning; but Chuka expected it, ducked under the vicious roundhouse right, and with Hahnsbach half-spun around, hit the Sergeant with a straight, driving right to the side of the jaw. Hahnsbach went down with a thud.

"Pretty good, gunslick," Hahnsbach said, getting to his knees. He dove for Chuka's legs, and both men went down, Hahnsbach on top of the younger man. He chopped a vicious left to Chuka's jaw, and then as he started to swing again, Chuka brought both legs up and lifted the Sergeant over in a flip and sent him sprawling. They got up and faced each other. Hahnsbach rushed in once more, swung another roundhouse right. Again Chuka ducked, swinging underneath and cracked the Sergeant in the ribs with all of his strength. Hahnsbach sagged. Chuka hit him again, driving his fist straight down onto the soldier's jaw.

Almost instantly, Chuka felt the power of a left hand dig him in the stomach as Hahnsbach started his backswing, and the Sergeant's brute strength carried through, though Chuka had already hit him. Both men went down, not unconscious; but neither could rise. They stared at each other across the short distance of ground that separated them.

"Do—I—" Chuka gasped out the words, "—still have to wait until later?"

Hahnsbach lifted his head. He did not get a chance to answer. The sharp, commanding voice of Captain Carrol stopped him.

"Sergeant!" Carrol's voice exploded. "What's the meaning of this?"

"Just a little Indian wrestling, Captain," Chuka said, as Jake came over to help him up.

"Sergeant?" Carrol demanded.

"That's all it was, Sir," Hahnsbach said. Several soldiers came forward to help Hahnsbach upright, but the big man pushed them aside.

"Mr. Watkins?" Carrol asked, speaking to Henry, who stood to one side. "Is that right?"

"Well, it was a kind of test of strength, you might say, Captain," Henry said.

"I see," Carrol said. "Report to Colonel Valois at once, Sergeant." Carrol then turned to Chuka. "Colonel Valois would also like to speak with you, Mr. Chuka. And you, Mr. Watkins and Mr. Crowford."

"I told you there wasn't any anger in this, Captain," Chuka said. "No need to make anything out of this. No harm's been done."

"This has nothing to do with your—" Carrol paused, "*Indian* wrestling, Mr. Chuka. It is another matter."

Chuka nodded and began to belt his gun and tie down the holster. Hahnsbach was brushing his uniform. When the two men were alone, Hahnsbach looked over at Chuka. "You would have made a fine soldier," he said, a lazy grin spreading over his face as he felt his jaw.

Chuka rubbed his stomach. "And you would have made a fine bull."

Hahnsbach grinned broadly as Chuka turned to follow Jake and Henry, with Carrol, walking toward Valois' quarters. Chuka could not stand up straight, still feeling the pile driving effect of Hahnsbach's left to the stomach. Hahnsbach bawled orders to his men to continue their stable detail and caught up with Chuka. "I didn't think you'd fight, gunslick."

"And you a soldier!" Chuka said, turning to look at the big man. "What have you learned, if you don't know a simple thing like never underestimating your enemy?"

By ten that morning, with no sign of Trent, Colonel Valois made his decision. In the early morning, he had walked along the north and west walls of Clendennon, several times climbing to the high north tower, searching the distant rims of the grass country with his field glasses. Aside from the wild game, nothing had move since sunup.

Alone at his desk, his orders to Carrol to round up the civilians and all officers of Clendennon still ringing in his ears, he studied a large scale map of an area extending for twenty miles around Clendennon. He was deep in concentration, chin resting on his hands, when the men entered his office.

He started speaking at once, without introduction. "Every one of you knows the country and the general area around Clendennon. Now there are ten of you—Mack, Daly, Carrol, Cook, Hahnsbach, Baldwin, Howard, Watkins, Crowford and—ah—Chuka. I want each of you to take one trooper and go to the appointed areas I have marked off here on the map. Search for one hour, penetrating as far as you can, then turn back, retracing your own trail to the Fort." Valois spoke in a crisp, direct manner, holding up the map and pointing to the ten different sections dividing the large area around Clendennon. One by one, he pointed to an area and then to a man, describing how he wanted the search made. When he came to Chuka, the gunfighter held up his hand.

"Just a minute, Colonel," Chuka said easily.

"Yes?" Valois said sharply, caught up by the sudden interruption.

"I don't know about Jake and Henry here; but I got business in Montana. And riding out for you, well, I'd just rather not ride this morning."

Valois cut in, as if he had not heard. "Do you know this country?"

"I do."

"Then you will take this area here," Valois said. "Now each of you—"

"Colonel—" Chuka said.

Valois looked up again, irritation in his manner and voice. "Yes, what is it?"

"I said I'd rather not ride this morning."

Valois looked at Chuka a long time then dropped the map. "You are an experienced man—"

"Probably the most experienced man in this room," Chuka said, cutting in, as Valois had cut in on him.

"You can be of valuable service—"

"One scout, more or less, won't make much difference—"

"That's not for you to decide—"

"It sure as hell is."

"I'm the commander here—"

"You don't command me, Colonel. The last man who told me to do something and I did it when I didn't want to, was my father."

"Are you refusing?"

"I am. I'll hang back and protect the women—with you."

"You're under arrest. Major Cook, disarm this man and put him into—"

"No, uh-uh. Major Cook isn't going to try anything foolish like that—"

"Major!"

"Nobody else either; unless they want to go right now." Chuka's voice came out hard and flat, perfectly controlled even.

"*Major!*" Valois said quickly.

But Valois had hardly spoken, and the Major had moved but a few inches, when Chuka made a slight motion with his right hand and the barrel of the .44 was aimed at Major Cook's stomach. "Don't move. Don't think about it, just ease off," he said carefully.

No one moved in the small office. No one breathed. Valois' eyes blazed, but he was in control of himself and that, more than any other detail, moved Chuka to hair-trigger alertness. "All right, Major," Valois said finally, with an air of resignation.

Cook started to back away. Chuka brought the gun upward.

"*I said, don't move!*" He said through his teeth. Major Cook looked at Valois, but he did not move.

Chuka took three steps back, then slipped his gun into the holster. He stood, slouching to his right side, his fingers only inches away from the butt of the gun. He looked at Valois. "I said I wouldn't ride for you, Colonel; and I mean what I say."

Valois fought for control of his voice. "This is a military post of the United States Army and I am the commanding officer."

"Yes, it is," Chuka said slowly. "And you're the boss. But I ain't to be commanded."

"As long as you are on this post, you will do as I *say*," Valois said coldly.

"In that case, Colonel Valois, I'll just get my pony and mosey along. But you ought to know that if you was half as smart as you think you are, you'd let Jake and Henry and me take the women and get the hell out of your fort right now."

"You are not allowed to leave this post, Mr. Chuka."

"You going to stop me?" Chuka asked.

"I can see to it that you are stopped," Valois said.

"Sure, go ahead and try it. You do that, Colonel. You send 'em after me, and try to stop me."

"If you resisted, I would have you shot."

"*You* wouldn't have nothing. You wouldn't be around to order anything. Good God, man, what do you think this—a game?"

"Mr. Chuka, I am giving you a direct order. If you try to leave this post against my orders, I'll hunt you down."

The shiny Colt .44 came out again, and with it, Chuka moved in a fluid, effortless motion to Valois' side. The blue steel barrel was rammed hard into the side of the young Colonel before anyone in the room could move.

"You wouldn't dare," Valois said arrogantly.

"Breathe easy, sonny, or I'll blow your tail off."

"Sergeant!" Valois shouted.

"Hold it, Sarge," Chuka warned. "You know I'm not kidding. Now just back it off. I don't want to do it. Don't jam me up."

Hahnsbach stepped back and dropped his hands.

Chuka spoke in Valois' ear. "Colonel, I don't want trouble. I've already pulled this weapon twice without using it. Maybe we're all lucky because of that. Now I'm going to put it away and walk out of here. I'm going down to the stables and get my horse and saddle and ride out. If you want to send six good men after me, then I guess you'd better start picking out six you don't like. I'll kill the first son of a bitch that tries me out. Remember that, Colonel, *I'm one of the best*, and I'll get an even half dozen before you get me."

Once more, Chuka stepped back, and looking at the faces of the men in the room, rolled the gun and eased it into his holster. He waited, but no one moved. He looked at Jake and Henry. Jake's indrawn, bitter look bore down on Chuka. Their eyes locked and held.

"You goin' now, Chuka?" Jake asked politely. He held the carbine level with the floor and put his arm on Henry's shoulder. "What you say we go now, huh Henry?" He said in a soft and friendly way.

"Fine," Henry said, his right hand resting easily on the butt of his .45.

Chuka stepped to the door; Hahnsbach blocked it. With his back to the others, Chuka faced the big Sergeant. "How about it, Sarge?"

Hahnsbach did not flinch. He looked past Chuka to Valois, and for a moment, the two soldiers looked at each other. Finally Valois nodded.

Hahnsbach stepped aside. Chuka smiled, turned to Jake and Henry. "Coming?"

The three of them stepped from the office together, and at the last moment, Chuka turned back to Valois. "Luck to you, sonny," he said.

Outside, Chuka looked at the two men. There was no need to say anything. Jake and Henry had said it all in the office when they backed him up. "Suppose, we get on along, huh?" Chuka said matter-of-factly.

Jake and Henry nodded, and the three of them started toward the stables. Chuka stopped at the mess room, collected their gear, and in a few moments was saddling his horse. His movements were quick and sure as he handled the leather. Jake and Henry waited for him at the entrance, holding their horses' leads, saddled, ready, watchful.

"Morning, Mr. Sheppard," Jake said. Chuka turned to see the man approaching him.

"That conference?" Sheppard asked, watching Chuka double-cinch the Texas saddle. "Then the situation is serious?"

"It could be. And then again, it could be nothing more than an Army scout sleeping off a drunk somewheres," Chuka said. He turned and gave the man a reassuring grin. "It's been known to happen you know."

"Oh, then you're leaving now?" Sheppard said, disappointment in his voice.

"Yup. We got business in Montana," Chuka said, looking at Jake.

Sheppard's face brightened up. "Business? What's it about?" But Chuka's hard look stopped the inquiry cold.

"Forgive me, Chuka. I'm nervous. And you seemed to be a man who knows, and I wanted to talk to you."

Sheppard hesitated. "There was something I wanted to say."

Jake and Henry turned away to give them privacy.

"About what?" Chuka asked, checking the cinch and the gear.

"Evangeline."

"Eve—what about her?"

"Well, I may be only a drummer, but I am a very observant man. I guess you might say that I am as successful a drummer as I am because I am observant. What I mean is, in my line of work, traveling around, meeting new people constantly, having to get their confidence fast, so you can at least show them your goods for sale, has sharpened my—eye for human nature."

Chuka waited, watching the man before him, listening, pulling the carbine from the boot and checking it.

"Yeah, I can see how you would have to be pretty shrewd at knowing people all right," Chuka said agreeably. "But what's all this got to do with Eve?"

"Just this—Sheppard said. "I've been too much on the run, selling, traveling, running, selling, to think much about settling down. But it came and I picked Eve. I don't know why. I knew about her. Met her more than a year ago in Trinidad. When I got back this time—well, I had intended to ask her to marry me; but I lost my nerve and I passed out. Luckily for me, she had selected me for a sucker and a quick skinning and a way to get out of Trinidad—"

"I know all that."

"What you don't know is this," Sheppard said. He turned away from Chuka and looked out over the Fort.

"This morning, when Major Cook and the Spanish ladies and I went for a walk around the Fort, you and Eve remained behind." Sheppard turned and looked at Chuka. "I don't know what you two talked about; and I don't care. I don't want to know. All I know is this: since Eve and I have been married, she made no bones about—how she felt about me. But this morning after talking to you, she—she—"

"Yeah?" Chuka asked cautiously.

"She is completely different. I think we might have a chance for something, Chuka—and in some way, you were the important difference—"

"You want me to tell you what we talked about?" Chuka asked.

"No—I don't want to know."

"Afraid?"

"Why should I be afraid. She's a different woman. Nothing you could tell me would make me feel any differently. I'm thankful, Chuka—thankful. And I just wanted you to know."

Chuka smiled. "Sure, Johnny," he said softly, "and I couldn't be happier for you. Eve's a damn fine woman. So when—"

Chuka froze. There was a noise behind them, deep in the back of the stables. Chuka slipped to the wall and pulled out his six-gun. He rocked back the hammer. "All right! Come out of there!" Chuka commanded.

Nothing moved. Sheppard looked at Chuka. "I didn't hear anything."

"Shut up!" Chuka said. He moved into the stables, easing around the stalls, looking in, gun up and ready. "I said, come out of there!"

Sheppard shrank to the opposite side of the log building and watched. From the depths of the stable, there was a stirring and rustling in the hay. Slowly, not clearly at first, there emerged the dark leather shift of an Indian woman's dress, then the face. Her expression was one of fright—bordering on terror. Her eyes were on Chuka and the gun, then she discovered Sheppard and her eyes opened wide with fright. She shifted her gaze back to Chuka and the gun. Jake and Henry discovered the confusion and came in; Jake with the carbine up and Henry pulling out the .45. The woman's movements were quick and jerky now that she was facing four of them. She looked like something wild.

"Well, I'll be damned!" Henry said.

"My God!" Sheppard breathed.

Chuka advanced on her slowly, still holding the gun aimed at her. The Indian woman retreated a few steps.

She turned and looked for a way to escape through the rear. And then, suddenly, she turned and moving as swiftly as an animal, ducked her head and threw herself forward, trying to escape past them. Jake grabbed her and then all three men held her down tightly, while Sheppard brought them a rope. When the woman was tied, hands behind her, they picked her up and stood her on her feet. "Is she a spy?" Sheppard asked.

"Naw, she isn't a spy. Some trooper probably slipped her in here at night and hid her up in the hayloft." The woman suddenly jerked the rope and nearly escaped from them; but Chuka caught and held her. She spit in his face. Chuka slapped her so hard, he knocked her down.

"*Winas to mayo*," she said through her teeth.

"She's a Ute," Chuka said. Jake and Henry agreed. Jake grinned.

Chuka looked at him. "I know, she called me son of a dog wolf." Chuka jerked the rope and half-pulled the woman through the doorway into the open parade grounds. "All right, Pocahontas, let's see what Colonel Valois will look like when he sees you."

Jake and Henry and Sheppard followed close behind. They were spotted at once. The troopers stopped in their labors to gawk at the group, the Indian woman twisting her hands trying to escape. With Chuka holding the rope and the woman before him, they had stopped a few feet away from the entrance to the office when the door opened and Valois, followed by the others, stepped out of the building. Valois stopped, stared and remained perfectly still. "What's the meaning of this! Who is this woman?" He demanded.

"There you go again," Chuka said. "I'll swear, Colonel, you just don't seem to understand that *everybody* won't spit when you say hawk."

Valois ignored Chuka and swung his gaze to Sheppard.

"What do you know about this, Mr. Sheppard?"

"She was hiding in the hayloft. She tried to escape—Mister Chuka caught her."

Valois stepped of the gallery and approached the woman. "What is your name, woman?" Valois demanded.

The woman shrank back.

"She's a Ute. Probably don't understand you, Colonel," Henry Watkins said.

"Can anyone here speak her tongue?" Valois asked, looking around in back of him. No one moved.

"Trent could, Sir, if he was here," Lieutenant Daly said.

"But he isn't here, Lieutenant," Valois said.

Sheppard licked his lips. "She spoke to Mister Chuka—and he understands her."

"Is that true?" Valois asked. "Do you speak her tongue?"

"True," Chuka said.

Valois' face turned blood red. He glared at Chuka.

His jaw worked. "Has she—indicated—what she is doing here—in Clendennon?" Valois asked, trying hard to control his anger.

"No," Chuka said. "She just called me the son of a dog wolf—"

"Nothing else?"

"Colonel, if you'd get yourself another rope, I'll take mine and go on about my business. Only reason I tied her up like this was to keep her from scratching my eyes out." He moved up behind the woman and began to untie the knot. "She's a hellcat."

Valois' face was beet red. "Mr. Chuka," he said, in a voice that was trembling with restraint, "I ask you, for the sake of the lives of the people at Clendennon, to cooperate and question this woman and act as interpreter."

Chuka stopped untying the rope binding the woman's hands and looked at Valois. He stepped back and nodded. "She ain't nothing but a whore one of your troopers sneaked in. She won't tell you anything."

"Ask her how long she's been inside the fort," Valois said. Chuka quickly looked up at him. "Please," Valois added heavily.

Chuka nodded. He spoke to the woman. She replied.

He spoke to her again. They exchanged words in the language of the Utes, Chuka speaking fluently and easily.

"She says she's been here since the last moon."

"Last moon?" Valois repeated.

"Nearly a month," Chuka said.

"How did she get here—who brought her?"

"I asked her that. She won't tell."

"If she's been here a month, she could have been sending out information."

"I don't think so," Chuka said. "What's there to know about this place that's so special? It's pretty common knowledge that you've got only about forty men here—no heavy cannon—"

"Do you believe her?" Valois asked.

"Yeah," Chuka said. "I believe her. She's just a poor starving Injun squaw that took the first opportunity that came along to get a square meal." Chuka shook his head. "She musta been pretty hungry though. This ain't ordinary for a Ute woman."

The woman listened to the conversation, her head turning from Valois to Chuka. She spoke to Chuka. He replied.

"What did she say?" Valois asked.

"Well, you don't have to worry about her. She just asked me if we were going to return her to her people."

"No," Valois said. "We'll keep her here."

"I already told her that. She wants to stay. If she goes back to old Hanu's camp, her own people will cut off her nose for having anything to do with the white man."

"Do you believe her?"

"Yeah, they'll cut off her nose, then kill her."

Valois looked around at Henry and Jake. Henry nodded. "That's what'll happen to her, all right. If you turn her out now, she'll be dead before sundown."

"All right, put her in the guardhouse," Valois said.

"And see that she's given something to eat—and extra blankets. She must be frozen in nothing but that skin she's wearing."

The woman sensed a decision had been made. She turned and spoke to Chuka, who replied. She started to lunge against the rope, trying to escape.

"What is it now?" Valois asked, when the woman had been restrained.

"She thinks you're going to kill her," Chuka said.

"Well, explain to her that we're not—"

Chuka looked at the troopers who had gathered. "One of you has been feeding this woman and taking care of her. Now why don't you step out and make it easier for her to understand—"

Not one man moved.

"Dammit!" Chuka exploded. "Somebody's been taking care of her. She musta meant something to you, if it wasn't anything but—" he stopped quickly when he saw Helena Chavez standing to one side, listening.

After a moment, Chuka addressed the men again. "She's scared half to death."

Then from two different sides of the group surrounding Chuka and the woman, Helena Chavez and Evangeline Sheppard moved toward Chuka. Both of the women appeared to be startled to see the other. Then Evangeline smiled at the Indian, stepped forward, taking the rope from Chuka, and began to untie the knot. At the same time, Helena removed her cloak and draped it over the shoulders of the Ute. Then with the Indian woman between them, they walked through the group of men, into one of the buildings.

To one side, the proud figure of Veronica Klietz watched the scene with cold, emotionless eyes.

Valois turned to the men. "I will not press the issue now, except to say that the person, or persons, responsible for this have until sundown to present themselves to me—or there will be grave consequences."

No one stepped forward. Valois dismissed them. He turned to the officers, standing with Baldwin and Howard, on the gallery floor. "All right, gentlemen, you have your orders. Carry on."

Chuka had recoiled his rope and turned towards the stables, with Jake and Henry at his side, when Valois called to him. "Chuka—"

Chuka halted and turned slowly, waiting for Valois to catch up with him. "Are you still going to leave?"

"This isn't my fight, Colonel," Chuka said. "One, or two, or three more guns isn't going to make that much difference. And I've got a healthy respect for odds in my favor."

Chuka shrugged and turned away, Jake and Henry once more falling in beside him.

"Just a minute," Colonel Valois said.

Chuka stopped once more, and Valois hurried to his side.

"Would you leave the women here?"

"I already told you how I felt about that," Chuka said.

"I thought back there—with the Indian woman—" Valois said, "when you consented to act as interpreter—"

Chuka looked at him sideways. "I'm not a hard man to get along with, Colonel. But you're a soldier and that makes you look at things your way—I look at them differently. The same things. Differently."

"I wonder if I can believe that," Valois said seriously. "And what it implies."

"Why are you bucking so hard for me to see things your way, Colonel? You know what I am. Your mind's been made up since I rode in here."

"And what are you, Chuka?" Valois asked.

Chuka looked at Jake and Henry. "Man moving. Man with a gun. Man with a few friends—not many—but a few." His words came slowly and were drawn from sudden, deep introspection. For a moment, his words caught and held the three men listening to him. Each was moved. Jake broke his stare and walked away. Henry bit his lip. Only Valois continued to stare at Chuka. Suddenly the big man spoke. "Also, a man who has a hell of a lot of drinking and fighting and—and women to run though before I give over—"

The spell Chuka's words had cast upon them was broken. They started towards the stable where the scouting parties' scurry of activity caused Valois to stop. "Suppose I told you that—because you are what you are—you're the only man in this Fort that I feel could do the job I need done—and that I could rely on."

"Hahnsbach," Chuka said.

"He couldn't scout, and you know it."

"The stagemen—Baldwin and Howard—good men."

"They're not trained to survive at *all costs*—like you."

"That's true, Colonel; and I don't mind telling you that I'm surprised to see that you can tell the difference."

Valois hesitated. "I could scout. I could do it. But—I'm the commander here."

"Then you've got a hell of a problem, if you don't mind my saying so," Chuka said. "I'd better be getting on. The sun is high and I need to put space between me and your coming fight before the sun goes down."

"Then you won't stay?"

"You're making it hard for me, Colonel. I don't like to be all jammed up, like you're making it look. Regardless of what the Good Book says, all men are not equal. I'm alive today to prove it. You went after me the wrong way."

"Pride?"

"No, facts. And you know it. But for me to do anything for you now, I'd have to backwater. I'd rather it be you who did that. But you can't, because you're—well, you're Colonel Valois."

"All right," Valois said, "as you said back in my office, you're not to be commanded. But don't you see, just because you're not to be commanded, you're the man I need. And I believe the situation is critical."

"If you think that way, then you've got a lot more savvy than I figured you for. And you're right, the situation is critical."

"It isn't your fight. You don't have to stay," Valois said. "But there must be some way I can appeal to you."

Chuka was silent.

"There isn't a man here, aside from Hahnsbach, that wouldn't put a bullet in my back and run, if he dared."

"Then you really got problems," Chuka said.

Valois watched the scouting parties mount. "Let me ask you this. Do you think Hanu will attack?"

Chuka was slow in answering. "Your scout thought so, enough to go out at one o'clock in the morning."

"How well do you know this country?"

"I know it."

"Well?"

"I know it," Chuka said.

The scouting parties were mounted and ready to leave. Valois turned and looked at his men and horses. Chuka walked into the stable and began to replace the rope on his saddle. He started to mount and saw Valois staring at him.

"Is your gun for hire?" Valois asked.

"To who—and for what—and for how much?" Chuka asked, mounted, the horse standing perfectly still.

"To me," Valois said, personally.

"Not the Army?"

"To me."

"What kind of job?"

"Scout."

"Hanu?"

"Find out if there is going to be an attack."

Chuka thought about this. "How much?" He asked.

"What are your prices?"

"It usually depends on how much I think I can get. But not—always."

"How much?"

68

"Well now—that depends," Chuka said.

"On what?"

"When I hire on—it isn't usually just to sit and drink coffee."

"Meaning?"

"I do things my way. Not the Army way—or your way. My way."

"What would be your way—in this case?" Valois asked.

"First off, you'd call off that army of scouts you've got ready to ride, that couldn't scout their way out of a gopher hole—with the exception, maybe, of Baldwin and Howard."

"All right. Anything else?"

"I wouldn't want to risk my own animal. I would need four of your *best* horses."

"Anything else?"

"I'd want one thousand dollars before we do anything else."

"Will you take my marker?"

"No."

"You doubt that I would pay you?" Valois asked, his voice tightening up.

"No. If you owed me, Colonel, I'd collect. But if you're not alive, I don't see how I could collect from a dead man," Chuka said evenly. "It's a cash deal. In advance."

Valois hesitated a moment. "Will you sign a voucher?"

"Will it obligate me to anything?"

"It will mean that I have given you Government money, and you received it—to do a job."

"Then I'll sign it," Chuka said. "You'd better hurry up, Colonel. We ain't got much time."

"Meet me in my office in five minutes," Valois said. At that moment, Major Cook rode up and saluted Valois. "Detail ready to move out, Sir."

"Dismiss the men," Valois said. "Pick out four of the best horses we have." He turned to Chuka. "How do you want them—"

"I'll take care of that."

Valois nodded and headed back across the parade grounds. Henry and Jake cased up alongside Chuka. "Why are we going to need four horses, Chuka?" Henry asked.

"I been trying to figure that out myself," Jake said.

"We," Chuka said, "means just me. I'm going to run 'em bow-legged for speed."

"Now wait a minute," Henry said. "You going out there by yourself?"

"Take one of us," Jake said. "You and me are the lightest riders—"

"Hold on, Jake—" Henry said.

"Both of you step back," Chuka said with a grin. "I'm going alone. And don't argue with me. You haven't said anything about the deal I made with him."

"Deal?" Jake said, and Chuka could tell that the man was totally unaware of the cash involved.

"Do you have any money?" He asked the two men. He knew they didn't. There wasn't twenty dollars between them.

"Well, I had some money back in Trinidad, but you got there a little too late. I blew it in at the Casino on a real good time. I got about sixty dollars, silver. When we go back to Montana, now aren't we going to need some spending money to handle little things like grub and a hotel room?"

"But goddamit, Chuka—" Jake began to explode.

Chuka waved him away. He saw Valois standing in front of his office. "You can help me plenty by picking out four of the finest beauties this Army has got, strip 'em down to the neck leather. Get me a canteen of fresh water—and hurry it up."

A few minutes later, inside Valois' office, the young Colonel opened a safe and removed a cash box. Chuka eyed the money. "I should have said two thousand," he said.

"Hedging, Mr. Chuka?"

"No—I gave you my price and you met it," Chuka said. "But a man will do rash things sometimes."

"What is your name?" Valois asked, inking his pen.

"Chuka."

Valois looked up. "Just Chuka?"

"Nobody would know who it was if I told you my real name. Chuka's good enough."

"Sign here."

Chuka took the pen and signed.

A few minutes later, the money tucked into his pocket, Chuka and Valois stepped out onto the gallery. Four sturdy horses, bare-backed, three of them roped together, stood at the hitch. Jake and Henry stood to one side. Chuka walked over to his own horse and removed the short-barreled carbine from the boot, cut a three-foot length of rope from his lariat and tied a sling onto the rifle. He slung it over his shoulder, slipped the canteen strap over his arm and then turned to the horses. He went over each animal carefully, feeling the legs, particularly the knee, shank and pastern. Finished with his examination, Chuka swung onto the back of the free animal, and took the lead rope from Jake. He looked down at Valois. "When I come back, I'll fire three shots for trouble. Just one if everything is all right."

"How long will you be?"

"If I'm not back in three hours, send Jake and Henry out to help, and then buckle your belts." Chuka grinned at Valois. "*I've* got all the help I need, Colonel. One thousand dollars."

Major Cook, who had stood to one side observing the scene quietly spun around. "Sir! Are you sure you can trust this man not to steal the horses—and take the money and run off? He is an admitted coward. He refused to go earlier. It appears to me that it's an attempt at—"

Chuka kicked the horse in the flanks and spurted to the Major's side. He brought up his right leg, without warning, the toe of the Texas booth catching Major Cook under the chin. The vicious kick sent Cook sprawling, blood flowing freely from his mouth. Chuka looked down at him. "Now if you want to do something about that, you lying son of a bitch, you just bought yourself a chance when I get back?"

He looked around at the men—lastly at Valois. "You want to change your mind about our deal, Colonel?"

"No," Valois said instantly.

Jake and Henry moved away from the crowded scene as Chuka swung the horses around and were a few feet away from the others when Chuka passed them by. He looked down at them. "Now you do right by getting help if I don't get back. That Colonel, he's got savvy. And you take care of yourselves, heah?" He waved them away and rode on, passing the officers' quarters where the Indian woman had been taken. Helena had watched the scene from the window. Chuka slowed his horse to a walk, raised his hat and nodded. "Ma'am," he said politely, "take care, now."

She followed the rider on the bare-backed horse through the small gate, until he was out of sight.

"Nobody is close to him," Evangeline said at Helena's side. The young Spanish-Mexican woman spun around. "Back in Trinidad he spent his money like a drunken miner. There wasn't one of the girls at the Casino that wouldn't crawl to be his girl. But none of them were. Nobody got closer than—" She stopped and looked at Helena.

"I understand," Helena said warmly. "Do you think he will come back?"

"Honey, if he's alive, he'll be back," Evangeline said.

Neither of them had noticed the approaching figure. "Helena!" Señora Klietz said.

Helena turned quickly, paled. "*Si, madama?*" The coldness between them had not been modified since the night before.

Señora Klietz's tone or manner did not change. "How is the Indian woman?" She asked, entering the room, brushing past both Eve and Helena. "The poor wretch!" Veronica Klietz said. "Men! They are pigs— look at her. No telling what she has had to suffer at their hands. Come! Get this animal skin out of my sight. Helena, go to our trunks and get clothes for her—the dark blue silk I bought in Madrid. Hurry now!"

Helena flew from the door. Veronica Klietz turned to Evangeline Sheppard. "Do you think she will permit us to wash her?"

Eve grinned. "We can try; but it won't be easy."

"Look at her eyes. She's frightened to death. Come—come now," Veronica Klietz said gently as she approached the Ute woman. "Men!" She added with contempt. "Pigs—"

"They sure are," Evangeline Sheppard said, then under her breath, "Sometime—"

"What was that?"

"I said they sure are, just give them time," Eve replied.

72

Valois stepped from his office half an hour later to see Sergeant Hahnsbach supervising six troopers carrying steaming water in large tubs across the parade grounds.

"Sergeant!" Valois demanded. "What's the meaning of this!"

"It's for the Spanish ladies and Mrs. Sheppard, Sir. They're—" The big Sergeant's eyes opened wide. "They're going to give the Indian woman—a bath, Sir!"

In a military post as isolated and as removed from even the semblance of normal frontier duty as was Clendennon, the ordinary became the extraordinary, the gossip was usually hardened fact, the squadroom bull session, a beginning for a rebellion.

Of all the hard cases that were forwarded to Valois' command, of all the toughs, recalcitrants, malingerers, the unruly and ungovernable that made up the force of Clendennon, none was more cunning and clever and with less conscience than Theodore Spivey.

Spivey was a short, hawk-faced soldier whose uniform always looked too large for him, who never combed his hair, and shaved only when Hahnsbach stood over him and threatened to throw him into the guardhouse unless he did so. He had thin, long hands that were as adept at picking pockets as they were at handling a gun. There were only two men at Clendennon who could outshoot Spivey, and though Hahnsbach had proved it over and over again, Valois had refused to shoot against Spivey in a match contest. Valois did not refuse for fear of losing; but rather, he did not want to give Spivey an opportunity to overstep his station, which Valois had recognized early, Spivey was eager to do. Spivey came from the South. The bastard son of a penal colony guard in Georgia, without the care of a mother, Teddy Spivey grew up under the influence of a father, who, only by a stroke of fate, had been placed in charge of the prisoners, rather than being one himself. At the age of six, Teddy knew how to pick locks. At ten, he was running for a grog house. At twelve he had killed his first man. Fourteen found him a prisoner in the selfsame penal institution where he had been raised, under the rule of his father, who was still a guard. It was not difficult for young Teddy to find a way of escaping; but he refused to do so until he had exhausted every penny from the other prisoners with the promise that he would lead them to freedom.

With the money and a promise that he would return and set things straight for them, Spivey turned to his father, who negotiated a pardon for his son on the strength of information of a mass escape. Seven were killed in the attempt. Four died later of wounds. Teddy Spivey, just turned fifteen, had stood on the walls of the prison and helped the guards shoot down the would-be escapees.

The war of secession had begun, and Spivey gravitated into the Army, first for the South, joining the Georgia 17th, then deserting to join the Pennsylvania 4th, when he saw, with his cunning and shrewd instinct for survival, that the South was losing the conflict.

From petty theft to one serious felony after the other, Spivey moved in his Army career, his gift of speech always clearing him when charges against him were specified. Finally there was murder—and though he was able to talk his way out of a sentence and hanging once more, the Army had had just about enough of him. He was to be discharged. But at that time Clendennon had been set up, for the purpose of sending difficult soldiers to that distant post, and Spivey was the first to arrive there. He was, with the exception of Hahnsbach and Valois, the oldest in point of service at Fort Clendennon.

Theodore Spivey, quickly and accurately, sized up the situation at Clendennon. He knew Valois was a commander that would take none of his guff, Sergeant-Major Hahnsbach would knock him on his ear if he should so much as step one inch out of line, and escape was impossible. Spivey had, characteristically, waited for others to try to escape over the grass flats before he himself tried. When he saw that even the toughest, boldest, cleverest of them were brought back slung over the back of a horse, either dead or in chains, Spivey gave up the idea of escape and decided to wait for his time to run out.

Rumors at Clendennon, in the squadrooms, were usually started by Ted Spivey. But it was not just ordinary gossip, retelling of something overheard, or made up. When Spivey planted a rumor, it was usually with an eye to serve his end. It was just so when, lingering behind in his duties in the stable detail, he had overheard the full conversation between Chuka and Valois.

Here was something for a man looking out for himself to consider fully. He slipped away from the stables and hurried to his secret hiding place, down behind several bales of hay in the south sally port. Three shots would mean trouble, one shot meant everything was all right.

He considered everything very carefully, taking in the fact that Valois had not allowed the stage to continue to Granada, that Lou Trent had not returned, and that Valois had, in so many words, backed down before the gunfighter.

This, more than any other fact in his considerations, convinced Spivey that it was time for him to start thinking seriously about getting out of Clendennon and saving his own neck.

But just running off himself, if Hanu was out there, would be like jumping from the frying pan into the fire.

How?

He sat a long time, his forehead scrunched in thought, his hands nervously picking at the straw hay in the bales around him. It was some time before Theodore Spivey aroused himself, his plan fully conceived, and his moves calculated to bring about the satisfactory deliverance of one Theodore Spivey, along with the money from the safe in Valois' office.

Slipping out of his secret place, careful to avoid Hahnsbach and not be seen by Valois, he made his way to the officers' quarters and tapped on the window pane.

"What are you doing here?" Cook demanded.

"Ah gotta talk to you—it's urgent and important, Major!"

"What's the matter with you?"

"I'll be down at the sally port. In fifteen minutes," Spivey said, straightening, looking directly at the brutal bruise on Cook's face, where Chuka had kicked him.

No one appeared to notice Spivey's movements as the little man slipped back to the sally port and waited. He did not have to wait long before Major Cook appeared, looked around, and then slipped into the passage between the bales of hay.

"What's the meaning of this, Spivey?" Cook demanded. "What the hell's so urgent?"

"What you reckon old Hanu is going to do, Major?" Spivey asked.

"Did you get me out here to ask me that?" Cook turned on his heel and started away.

"Just a minute," Spivey said. "You'd better hope that Hanu does something—or we'll never get out of here."

Cook stopped and turned slowly. "What do you mean?"

"I mean, the only way we're going to bust that safe in Valois' office and get outa here is to have something big going on."

"Big—how big?" Cook said. "What good will it do if Hanu does attack?"

"I didn't say attack. I said do *something*. You think it would be hard to get the rest of these sore-headed soldiers to agree to running out of this place—with just the threat of an attack?"

Cook was silent. "Do you think you could talk them into it? Without Hahnsbach knowing?"

"Can you get into the safe?" Spivey asked.

"I can."

"Then I'll take care of the others," Spivey replied.

"But you're going to have to do the leading with them. I can rile them up; but they won't listen to me in the end. It would have to come from an officer."

Cook stared at Spivey. "I wish I had never gotten involved with you."

"It's too late for that now," Spivey said, with a snarl. "You should have thought about that when we brought that woman in here—and who's going to believe that I handled it all by myself, without some help from an officer? And there's a dozen of them soldiers that would swear you handled the whole thing."

Cook stared at his hands. "I ought to kill you right now."

Spivey backed up. "And what would that get you? Nothing but a rope—or a firing squad. Don't fool around with me. I already told a couple of the others what I planned. They'd know what happened if you tried anything like that."

Spivey suddenly changed his tone. His voice became soft and per-suading. "Look, Major, think of it this way. If we stay, the most we can come out of this with is a kick in the tail when our time is up. And if Hanu does attack, what the hell are we going to get out of it? Except an Arapaho arrow in the back—if we're lucky."

"What is your plan?" Cook asked.

"If Trent or the gunfighter comes back, there's a signal. Three shots if there's going to be trouble, one if it's all right."

Cook nodded.

"That's our signal. If it's trouble or not, we take over."

"I can see how we might get away with it, if Hanu does attack; but if he doesn't—"

"Then we get out there, and we make him attack. Only instead of coming back to the Fort, we just keep going. They burn it to the ground. And who will ever know what happened?"

"It might work—"

"And you get the money."

"There won't be much, after we divide it up with the others."

Spivey laughed through his nose. "How the hell did you ever get to be a Major? Who said we'd divide it with the others? They don't have to know anything about it-all *they* know is we're getting the hell out. The money is strictly between you and me."

"You're—the most evil thing I've ever seen in my life," Cook said, conviction rising in his voice.

"What about the others?"

"Others?"

"Captain Carrol and Mack and Daly—"

"Mack might go along with us, but I doubt Carrol and Daly would. They—"

"All right, the hell with them. We'll take care of anybody that stands in our way."

Spivey worked his way to the end of the sally port and looked out. He motioned for Major Cook to leave. "Remember," Spivey said, "right after the gunfighter and Trent come back—"

"And if they don't?"

"Then that means for sure that Hanu is going to attack; and we move at sundown. That way, we'll have a full night of darkness for cover."

Spivey pushed Major Cook from the sally port and shrank back into the protection of the bales. He watched the man retreat across the parade grounds, then smiling to himself, hurried out and walked toward the main squadroom.

Chapter Six

FROM the moment Chuka left the protection of the Fort, he rode the sturdy Army horse at a pressing gallop, riding in a straight line toward the cover of a nest of rocks that lay just beyond the rim of the plains surrounding Clendennon. He drove the first horse as hard as the animal would go, urging it to greater and greater speed. He tore into the rocky ledge at a full gallop. Once inside, he pulled up sharply, slipped from the back of the animal, and in the same rhythm, using his forward motion, ran up the side of a high peak of rock and earth. He stopped just short of the top, fell flat to the ground and inched his way forward the last few inches until he could see over the peak. From his height, he spotted the far, outer edge of the rocky development and the long sweeping plains beyond.

He saw movement, at once, as he had expected, brought up the carbine, took a deep breath, set himself. A pair of Indian ponies were just breaking clear of the rocks. He aimed, setting himself, judging for a lead shot and squeezed the trigger. A moment later, he saw the target move upward, toward him, then suddenly lurch and fall.

Chuka expected the second Indian to stop, and he did, but only momentarily. Then the brave broke out into a zig-zag pattern across the plains; but Chuka was no longer watching. By the time the Indian was on his second jog, racing away, Chuka had mounted a fresh horse, grabbed the leads on the remaining two and started from the rocky clutch at a gallop. He was beyond the rocks and onto the grass in less than a minute; then he was out on flat level ground, urging the horse.

He pulled his .44 as he drew near the fallen Indian, intending to throw a finishing shot into the brave; but he saw clearly that his carbine shot had taken the man between the shoulders, and put away his gun. He gained on the Indian ahead of him, picking up half the distance between them in a matter of minutes. Suddenly the horse beneath him gave out, and Chuka called up one of the remaining horses, shifting over to the third animal that ran, easily, alongside him. Still holding the last horse, and on the fresh one, Chuka pressed on, harder and harder. The Indian's pony was beginning to falter after a ten-minute hard gallop. Turning around, the brave saw that Chuka had nearly caught up to him.

The Indian slipped to the ground, rolling in the grass, hard; but he came up on his feet and stood poised a moment, perfectly still, and watched Chuka come in on him.

Then the brave dropped to his knee, pulled up a carbine, took level aim and fired.

But Chuka was not on his horse. He was also on the ground, heard the crack from the carbine as he went down, rolling, and heard the horse fall to the ground with a terrific force. Now there were only a hundred yards separating Chuka and the brave. When the gunfighter came out of his roll, he had the .44 in his hand. He sat back on his legs and fanned the big gun four times at the brave who was just sighting on him for a second shot.

The four slugs were thrown in a reasonably straight line, and in one second flat. Two shots went wild. Two of them tore into the brave — one in the head, one in the chest. He was dead before Chuka moved from his position on the ground.

Chuka remained perfectly still, falling forward into the grass, as if he had been hit, and remained that way for a minute. Then slowly, he turned his head and swept the horizon. Nothing moved. In the distance, he could see the Indian pony cantering away — and nothing else.

Chuka moved, standing up straight, ignoring the skyline that came down to meet the grass fields. He concentrated on gaining the confidence of the one remaining horse, walking toward it, slowly, gently, coaxing it. The horse was nervous and tired. Though it had not carried Chuka's weight, it had run the full distance from Clendennon. The animal shied once, and then, after trotting a hundred feet, came to a standstill and watched Chuka approach him. All the while, Chuka spoke to the animal in a soothing, calming voice. "Whooa, hoss. Nice, hoss. That's it; just easy now, hoss. Nothing going to hurt you, pony —"

He gained the animal, soothed and petted it, quieting it, not taking the chance of mounting it right away and having it jerk out from under him. He talked to the horse and then, slowly, grabbing the leather, swung easily onto its back. The animal took the weight without rebelling, and Chuka turned around, spotted the Indian pony and went off after it. He rode more easily now, swinging along at an even trot. He had a long way to go, and to make it, he had to have the other horse with him.

After Chuka had secured the Indian pony, he glanced at the sun, judged about a half-hour had passed.

He set out again now, pressing the Army horse as much as the animal would go, trailing the Indian pony at his side, settling into a hard straight ride toward the northwest.

Chuka had worked his way well to the west when he found what he was looking for. A low chaparral of evergreen oaks, moved into it and slipped from the horse.

"Rest easy, hoss." Chuka said, patting the animal on the flank. Just stand and rest—get good and rested."

He securely tied the animal in a well-secluded thicket in the growth, then mounted the Indian pony and started working his way west. He crossed a hard crust of rocky field, topped a rise and looked down into a canyon that was half-filled with water during the spring thaw.

He had been gone from Clendennon a good hour by now. Chuka did not have much time. He had been climbing, gaining altitude steadily, since leaving the plains, and the air was thinner. He found an entrance into the canyon, the walls marked with glacial striation, deep scars of rocks, crushed forward by moving ice in some lost era, then deeper into the canyon, the more recent markings of water flow, tumbling huge rocks, and trees uprooted from the torrential snow-melt that roared to the grass country below. He gained the bottom of the canyon, its floor, frozen hardpan, as smooth as a billiard table and as hard as granite. He walked the Indian pony easily, the slight animal making no sound on the canyon floor. Chuka's carbine lay across his lap, his head and eyes moved constantly, raking the sides of the walls that hemmed him in, seeing everything from the floor to the towering heights. He missed no movement, no sound. He saw an eagle circling, heard the sudden thunder of hooves as some deer above him became frightened and slashed away. There were signs of wild life, but no sign of Indians, no sign of a sentry, and nothing to indicate that Lou Trent had come this way.

Yet Chuka was sure that Trent would come through the canyon on a probe of Hanu's camp. It was the surest trail, if a rider wanted to make time between Clendennon and the site of the Arapaho build-up on Rush Creek, and the same was true for the Indians on their move southwest. The canyon would save them miles of roundabout movement. The canyon was the place—the critical point; and there was no sign—no sign at all.

Chuka walked the entire length of the canyon, which seemed to him about a quarter of a mile long and as narrow as a hundred feet at some points. He stood finally at the far end, before a sharply angled hill rising up from the hardpan floor, the sides of the hill were covered with the brownish stems of mountain flowers, thick underbrush that was still a little green. He searched the trail carefully, and as he lingered, his mind went back to the two Indians he had caught and killed on the plains of Clendennon. They had not been sitting there enjoying the warm afternoon sun. They were watching the Fort, perhaps for signs of a patrol coming out, or a rider going after help—watching the Fort and waiting for the larger force to come. If that was true, Chuka reasoned, then Hanu's war party would be near at hand.

He studied the trail. Were there tracks?

Then he made up his mind. One rider had *gone up*—by himself—and two riders had *come down*. Lou Trent going up—and the two sentinels on watch back near Clendennon coming down.

There were two things that bothered Chuka now, like an itch that cannot be dulled. If Hanu prepared and planned an attack on Clendennon for that day, he would have to be quick about it. There was not going to be much time left for fighting.

The second and most important thing that the rider could not figure out, was why—with the passage of the canyon so wide open, with so many places for a sentry to hide and command the canyon—hadn't a sentry been posted.

Chuka had little doubt that, had such a sentry been watching him, he would have attempted to pick him off.

Then, suddenly, the gunfighter sensed the unseen.

He *was* being watched.

Chuka moved easily, slinging the carbine over his shoulder and held himself perfectly still, resisting a powerful impulse to wheel the pinto around and pound back down the canyon floor. He steadied himself, closing his eyes and summoned up the extra courage that always came when he was threatened with danger—something inside him seemed to take over and direct his movements, his thoughts and actions.

The sentries were there all right, and they had allowed him to ride clear to the very end of the canyon.

But *why*?

Then without being totally aware of what he was doing, in the impersonal way that his movements always were performed in moments of danger, Chuka knew *precisely* what to do. He moved.

But he did not wheel the pony around and pound back down the canyon passage. Instead, he urged the horse straight ahead, up the side of the hill, slapping the animal with his free hand, kicking it viciously in the belly with his boot heels, sending the startled, frightened mount in a digging plunge up the side of the slope.

Almost instantly the crack of a carbine sounded behind him, and seconds later the slugs tore into the frozen ground beneath him.

Twenty feet from the top of the rise, the Indian pony went down with a scream of pain as a bullet shattered its right front leg. Chuka fell sideways, throwing himself out, arms and legs spread-eagle to prevent himself from rolling back down the hillside. He scrambled to his feet and started digging for the top. He had the .44 out by then and stopped once to turn, trying to locate the enemy's fire. Chuka was instantly blinded by the sun. He threw himself to the side a split second before rifle slugs ripped into the ground at a spot where he had stopped moments before. He fought for the top of the slope.

Ten feet from the edge of the hill the faces of two Cheyenne braves, their hair drawn into even halves, bedecked with bands of colored beads and laying softly on their naked shoulders appeared before him. Chuka fired.

One went down with blood on his face. The remaining Indian fired coldly and deliberately, but missed. Chuka did not miss—and kept climbing.

He gained the top just as a third brave appeared. But Chuka had a foothold by then, and dove toward the Indian with all his strength as the Indian raised his rifle.

They went down together.

Somewhere in the back of his mind, as he wrestled with the Indian, Chuka sensed that the firing behind him had stopped. And he knew why. Those sitting on the towers of the canyon were not going to shoot and perhaps hit one of their own.

Chuka knew, upon his first contact with the Indian that he was going to win the struggle. The man was weak, and Chuka grabbed both wrists and locked his legs around the brave, at the same time twisting his body. They rolled together across the top of the rise for nearly thirty feet until they dropped into a shallow depression. Protected, however slightly from the fire of the sharpshooters on the canyon walls, Chuka freed one hand and grabbed the Indian by the throat. At the same time, he brought up his right knee sharply. The Indian's face twisted in pain. He was weakened; but he continued to struggle. Chuka brought up his knee once more. The brave was finished.

Chuka did not move. He lay as he was, the Indian and himself entwined. The body of the Indian was protection for him; and from this position, Chuka twisted his head to see where he was. He saw the horses, the tress a hundred feet away, and he saw Lou Trent, tied hand and foot, slumped at the base of a tree.

Keeping low, Chuka moved, setting his back against the side of the depression. He stripped the carbine from his back and turned in another attempt to locate the fire, coming down steadily from the canyon walls. The sun hit him again. It was useless. He couldn't see anything at all.

The reason why the Indians let him ride through the canyon without trouble became clear to Chuka now. They had wanted him alive. The figure of Lou Trent at the base of the tree assured him of this. There had been too many opportunities to kill him as he rode in for there to be another explanation. They had begun to fire on him only when he started up the hill. Chuka was certain that had he turned and ran back down to the canyon floor in a retreat, he would have been blocked by some barrier—and they would have had him.

All the time Chuka was working this out in his mind, his hands were working on the .44, reloading it. When he finished, he turned to the carbine, checking it for any sand or grit that might jam the firing mechanism. Both guns in working order, he concentrated on gaining the trees. There was no doubt in Chuka's mind that the Indians on the canyon walls realized he had defeated the brave, and they would be coming down after him. He did not have much time.

There was only one way to go, and that was straight ahead—across a hundred feet of open ground.

Naked to their gunfire for a hundred feet, and with the sun in his eyes, Chuka had no chance to return their fire.

His skin crawled as he stared over the short, one-hundred-foot stretch of dry, dead grass and wild flowers.

The firing behind him had slackened. There were not so many guns now. The Indians were coming down from their canyon perches. It would not take them long to get around in front of him—and then, goodbye, George.

"Can you hear me?"

It was Trent's voice.

"Yeah."

"Use the Injun," Trent shouted to him.

"Use the Indian?"

"Dammit, man. Pick up that Injun next to you and carry him on your back. It's the only chance you got."

Chuka moved at once, reaching out and pulling the unconscious brave to him. He slung the carbine over his arm, and pulled at the brave's limp form. Chuka got down low, and holding both of the man's arms across his own shoulders, the body of the Indian hanging like a sack upon his back, stood up.

"Now—*run!*" Trent roared at him.

Chuka began to run. The weight, while not much, was more than enough to make his steps unsure as he ran across the uneven ground.

The firing from the guns behind him increased in frenzy as Chuka stumbled forward. Then he felt the thump and the pressure of a slug entering the body of the Indian. Then another—and another. They were desperate now, and they fired at the struggling figure without care for the life of the Indian being carried.

"Keep coming boy—keep coming!" Trent yelled.

Chuka fell once. The slugs ripped into the ground, some of them tearing into the already dead body of the Indian, others missing Chuka by inches.

"Git up, dammit. Git up and keep coming," Trent bellowed.

Chuka pulled the Indian's body around once more, got underneath it and stumbled forward. He fell headlong into the protection of the trees, gasping for breath. With the last of his strength, Chuka crawled to Trent's side and slashed at the leather thongs that bound the scout.

Trent grabbed Chuka's carbine and dropped to one knee. He fired from the hip, spun sideways and fired into the thick brush. He killed the first Indian and wounded the second. The brave crashed through the brush, blood streaming from the shoulder. Trent pumped and fired twice in a blur of motion, catching the Indian in the chest. The Indian was thrown back onto the ground, twitched several times and lay still.

"The horses," Trent said calmly. "Take four—and cut the others loose."

Chuka struggled to his feet, still gasping for breath, and ran to the post to which the ponies were tied.

He grabbed the leads on the first four, held them and freed the re-mainder, firing his gun in the air to frighten them. The animals he held bucked and lunged, dragging Chuka to the ground; but he held on, and then Trent was at his side, taking the leads of two ponies from him.

"Let's go!" Trent yelled and leaped onto the back of the nearest ani-mal, kicking it hard. He cut through the trees to the northwest, not once turning around to see if Chuka was behind him.

There was no need. Chuka was only a few yards in back of the old scout, driving the Indian mount hard.

They broke clear of the trees, into a grassy dell. Trent headed for the bottom, hitting the ravine at a dead run, crashing through the un-derbrush without hesitation, ducking his head behind the horse's neck and driving forward.

They rode through the brush for a thousand yards, and at the far end of it, came out onto a stretch of table rock. Trent angled off to the western side of it, braked the forward movement of the pony, and dropped into a water cut that lead to the bottoms. Chuka recognized it as part of the plateau that surrounded the canyon. This was another way back to the glade and plains of the grass country.

The descent was sharp and treacherous. Trent's pony lost its footing and fell, both rider and horse rolling end over end to the rocky bottom. The man leaped up at the end of the fall. The horse stayed down.

Trent grabbed his second pony and swung onto the animal's back. Chuka shifted easily to the back of his fresh mount; and the two riders galloped past the rocky pits surrounding the bottom of the steep land-ing, out onto the open country. Trent headed in a straight southwest direction, his head down, his knees pinched onto the shoulders of the animal.

They were halfway across the plains that lead into the lower grasslands toward Clendennon when the Indian party appeared behind them.

The Indian's chased them for a mile or so; then pulled up and stopped when they realized they would never be able to catch the fleeing white men.

Only when Trent saw that the Indians were not going to press their pursuit did he slow down and wave Chuka to do the same. They came to a dead stop, slipped to the ground and stood in the hard, dry stubble of grass, turning to look back at the Indians, retreating to the higher ground. Their ponies were nearly exhausted from the hard run, but neither man paid attention to them. They continued to stare at the retreating group of Indians.

"That does it," Trent said.

"What?"

"Clendennon is going to get it, gunfighter."

"How far did you get?" Chuka asked.

"No further than where you found me. They were the advance party, waiting for Clendennon patrols, picked me up last night. I guess they been watching me as much as I been watching them. They knew just where I'd come, and how I'd make my approach. They got me good." The old scout shook his head. "It's time for me to quit cold when they can lay for me, and git me."

"How do you know Clendennon is going to be hit?"

"They been yammering all night. They know there's only a handful of men at Clendennon. They hoped to cut down the odds by boxing up the patrols in that canyon." Trent spun around and looked at Chuka, for the first time taking his eyes away from the point where the Indians were vanishing back into the high country. "What the hell are you doing out here, gunfighter? I never figured you to be one to take a risk—"

"I got paid," Chuka said.

"Paid?"

"One thousand dollars—to find out what's going on."

"*Valois—paid* you to scout for him?"

"Never mind that now," Chuka said. "Where's the main body of Hanu's braves?"

Trent's eyes clouded over, and he looked back at the spot where the Indians had disappeared. "That's just it, gunfighter—I don't know."

"Are you sure they're going to try anything?"

"They ain't going to try—they're going to do," Trent said coldly, his old eyes squinting. "Like I said, they talked all night. They plan to take Clendennon, and with the guns and supplies they get, fan out and arm every ragged-tailed Indian they can find. Sitting Bull's got Hanu so fired up, he thinks he can take everything back for the Indian, from west of the Mississippi clear to Denver."

Chuka said nothing. Trent looked at his pony, feeling it. "And, gunfighter, if he takes Clendennon and gets the supplies and guns without too much loss to his braves, he might go a long way before he can be stopped."

Trent swung onto the pony's back. "Come'n, these here animals will just about make it to the Fort before they cave in under us."

"How much time do you think we have?" Chuka asked, re-mounting his horse.

"Hanu's smart. He'll probe once before dark tonight, to see how things are going to be. The big show won't come until tomorrow morning." Trent slapped the pony. "Hikiyiii!"

The two riders broke out and began pounding for the long shadows that were now stretching out over the grass country.

When they broke away from the nest of rocks that were on the outskirts of Clendennon and were in plain sight of the Fort itself, Chuka drew his six-gun and fired three times.

There was no response from the Fort. Those within the walls of Clendennon heard the three-shot signal and watched the two riders with rising apprehension.

Chapter Seven

VALOIS sat behind his desk and listened to Trent's report, his officers and Sergeant Hahnsbach standing to one side. They all wore the same grave expression, all understood perfectly what the scout's report meant; and they believed it.

Valois closely questioned Trent and Chuka; but there was nothing either man could say that would alter the situation as Trent had outlined it.

When the interview was over, Valois stood. He took a deep breath. Chuka watched him set his teeth on edge. "All right," he said quietly. "That's it. Gentlemen," he said, turning to Daly, Mack, Carrol and Cook, "prepare Clendennon for an attack. We will carry out standing order number one and proceed with all haste. The women will be placed in a central building and serve as nurses to the wounded."

"Sir," Captain Carrol stepped forward, "the officers' mess, while not as central as some other buildings, is larger, and the water supply is closer."

"All right, we'll use the officers' mess as a hospital," Valois said. "That's all gentlemen. You know your jobs; you know what has to be done. Dismissed."

The men turned toward the door. Chuka and Trent started to leave. "Trent—" Valois said.

Trent stopped.

Valois looked at Chuka, then back to Trent. "What are the chances of getting—the women out safely?"

"No chance," Trent said instantly. "We oughta be hit in about an hour. Hanu's sure to have sent scouting parties over the whole area to make sure we don't have any help already coming in. They'd catch 'em for sure."

"You feel the same way, Chuka?" Valois asked.

"They'd be raped, scalped and dead before the sun went down," Chuka said.

"Apologies in order, Mr. Chuka?"

"No need for that, Colonel. It won't help the women."

"No," Valois said. He looked at both men. "Is there any chance of talking sense—"

Trent cut in, "You mean peace?"

88

"Yes, peace," Valois said. "I might consider surrendering—if there would be guarantees—"

Trent shook his head. "You got two chances, Colonel," the old scout said. "Put everyone on a horse and try to fight your way through to either Wallace or Garland—and burn the Fort and everything to the ground. Or stand and fight."

"You couldn't get Hanu to—call it off?"

"Colonel Valois," Trent said with formality, "the only thing that will satisfy Hanu and that bunch he's got with him is the hair of everyone here in the Fort."

"And the only thing to do is fight them?"

"You made the right decision, Colonel. If we're lucky, we might tear hell out of them and give them second thoughts—if we're lucky."

"Do I hear a note of reserve in your voice, Mr. Trent?" Valois asked.

"Yeah—you probably do. We ain't going to be lucky. We'd have to fight like a bunch of hungry, crazy, mad she-lions to do anything against them and have a chance. And with this gang—"

Valois did not hear the last part of Trent's statement. He cut in, his fist banging the desk. "Then we'll fight like a bunch of hungry, crazy, mad she-lions!"

"You got a bunch of strays, Colonel—cast-offs—They ain't soldiers like in Dodge or Wallace or Garland."

A sudden roar and the crack of a pistol from outside sent all three men racing to the door. Valois was the first to the outer door, Chuka and Trent behind them. All three men thought the attack had begun. They skidded to a stop. Sergeant Hahnsbach was holding Lieutenant Daly under the arms. Daly was bleeding from a large hole in his chest. Carrol, Mack and Cook whirled around and faced Valois.

Major Cook held his smoking pistol and brought it up.

"What's going on here?" Valois demanded.

The mob of men froze. No one moved.

"Major Cook—what's the meaning of this. Who shot that man?" He demanded.

"I shot him," Cook said. "And I'll shoot you, Valois, if you make another move. We're not going to stay here and get slaughtered for nothing. We're getting out!"

Chuka moved to one side, edging away, easily, catching the eyes of Jake and Henry, nodding slightly. All the time, his right hand hung loosely at his side, brushing the butt of the .44. Jake and Henry moved in opposite directions, and when Trent stepped away from Chuka, holding the carbine cradled in his arm, the four men had the thick clot of violence in a potentially deadly crossfire.

Valois was unaware of this. His whole attention was focused on Cook. "Major Cook, you are an officer of the United States Army—" Valois looked past him to the troopers standing as they had stood when Valois appeared in the door, "All of you are soldiers."

"We're *scum*—the *filth*—of the United States Army!" Cook shouted, his voice harsh. "You can fight Hanu and his crazy bucks by yourself, Valois."

Valois did not move. "Major Cook, I offer you a choice. Return to your duty and orders as they stand and prepare the men for an attack on this Fort—"

"*OR YOU'LL DO WHAT?*" Cook screamed, plunging the barrel of his pistol into Valois' stomach. "What will you do, Valois, if I don't?"

Valois ignored the gun in his stomach. He looked past Cook to the men crowded behind. "Listen to me," Valois shouted.

He took a short half-step forward, as if moving closer to the men, to address them, spun back suddenly, uncoiling his body like a bull whip, and using both hands separately, slapped the gun out of Cook's hand while he lashed him across the face with the other.

In that instant, two things happened. Chuka, Jake, Henry, and Trent leaped forward after Valois; and Valois himself stepped forward, kicking away the gun from Cook's outstretched hand in his crawling attempt to pick it up.

With Cook still down on his hands and knees, Valois stepped in and hit the man with a low, swinging right to the side of the face. The force of the blow, the sound of it resounding in the stunned silence, sent Cook sprawling backward.

Valois moved in. Cook turned and tried to dive for Valois' legs. At that instant, Valois side-stepped and brought both hands down, in a double fist, driving the blow into the back of Cook's neck. Cook went down, gasping for breath. He tried to rise. Valois stood before him, dropped his right side and hit Cook again, square in the face. Cook took the blow and with his own efforts to get up and the power of Valois' fist, came upright, staggering backward. Cook shook his head and cleared his vision.

He hunched forward, hands and arms outstretched like those of a wrestler, and began to shuffle in on Valois.

Valois moved forward to meet him. Cook lunged, and once more Valois moved aside, spinning around in a complete turn and hitting Cook again, with both his fists, in the back of the neck.

Cook made one more effort to rise. He struggled to his knees, arms stiffened, head hanging between his shoulders, and used the last of his strength to stand up. Valois loomed in front of him, watching every twitch in Cook's face. When Cook tried to swing again, Valois chopped him in the face with his left hand, vicious, wicked smashes that snapped back Cook's head. Valois swung from under his belt, his fist coming straight up from the ground. His right hand caught Major Cook in the left temple. Cook's body quivered once, was thrown slightly to the side in a half-spin and then crumpled to the ground, his body slack.

Valois turned slowly and faced the group of men. "Every one of you has been sent here to Clendennon because of some mistake in your past. There isn't one of you that can look me in the face and tell me you haven't wished a hundred times you could make up for that mistake. I can't promise you that your mistakes will not follow you once you leave Clendennon. But I know each man's record, and I know what each of you has done. And there isn't a man here that has done anything that comes close to being as yellow, as cowardly, as slimy as what you want to do now."

Valois stepped past Chuka and Trent and moved among the men. "But in case you don't care about that, in case there are few here that have no sense of decency at all and will run when they get the chance, let me tell you this—Hanu is out there. And so are more than four hundred of his braves. You wouldn't get further that the horizon before they would catch and kill you. But I doubt they would kill you right away. You are, most of you, experienced men. You can tell the others what to expect."

Valois stopped, closed his mouth and turned his back on the men, walking to the gallery before facing them again. "Your only chance is to fight the way you have been taught and trained. To use every trick and manner you know, or your soldier buddies know, to fight for your lives!"

Valois paused. "And then, in spite of this, we all may die. *There is no escape!*" Valois shouted suddenly. "Your only chance to survive is to stand and fight. There is only one way, and that is to fight with your head and your heart, to resist with all that is in you."

The faces of the men were unmoved. They were not going to be sold into the hands of death by speeches. Valois looked down at them, and realized this.

"Finally," he said, in a hard and flat and unyielding voice, "finally let me say this to you. You can leave. You can run. You can say to hell with Valois and the Army and Clendennon. You can let the young bucks in Hanu's band take the women; but to do this—you'll have to kill me first."

The men stirred.

"And," Valois said through his teeth, "I'm going to die hard."

"What happens to us afterward?" A man asked in the front ranks. "Suppose we do whip old Hanu and some of us are left, do we go on being treated like we had the plague?"

The men behind the speaker chorused their agreement with what had been said, pushing forward and demanding an answer. Valois held up his hands, high over his shoulders. The men became quieted to listen. Valois looked down into their faces.

"This is your chance," he said, "here, now. You want to return to your soldier buddies with honor—here is your chance."

"Is that a promise you're making?" A soldier demanded.

"I am your commanding officer," Valois said coldly. "Any man that proves himself deserving with get my support—*my full support.*"

The men fell silent again.

Valois stared at them. "Make up your minds."

Suddenly, amid the silence that followed as the men rolled the decision in their minds, Theodore Spivey shouted to them from the rear of the crowd. "Don't listen to him!" Spivey screamed. "It's the same old Army bunk you've been listening to—that them officers have been handing out—"

Spivey pushed his way to the front. He started up at Valois. "Look at him! He's making promises he never woulda made if he wasn't scared half to death that we'll run off and leave him here to face Hanu alone." Spivey turned his back on Valois and moved through the men. "How many times have you heard speeches like he just give you? How many times you heard an officer refuse to answer a question straight out—dodge behind fancy words. You asked him if we was going to be treated like dogs again, if we stood and fought—and what did he say? He said he'd give you his full support! Can you believe him? Can you— after what we've been through"

Spivey spun back to face Valois. "I say he's a chicken-hearted yellow dog that wants to hide behind us—"

Theodore Spivey never said another word. Valois' pistol was smoking, the sudden explosion of the pistol shot ringing in the air when the men, stunned, turned to look at Valois.

"I told you," Valois said, "that I would give any man that deserved it my full support. Make up your own minds. Nobody speaks for a soldier. He speaks for himself."

The bull-throated roar of Sergeant Hahnsbach shook the air at that moment. The men snapped around, yielding to the voice of authority by instinct, fear, a little training and, most of all, by years of iron discipline.

"Compannnnnyyyy! Ten-shunnnn!"

The men shifted in their tracks, half of them coming to attention instantly, others not so fast. Hahnsbach was in the middle of the men at once, pushing and shoving them around in a burly and gruff manner, showing not the least bit of restraint or lack of confidence. "Stand up there, Johnson! Brown! Ho! Mike, what are you doing?" And on through the group, until the men were in military order. "Full dress— dress it up—dress it up!"

Pushing, shoving, bawling Hahnsbach used his immense bulk and heavy-handed authority to sustain Valois' emphatic control after the cold-blooded shooting of Spivey.

Valois remained as he was, watching, seeing, knowing the crisis had passed. When the men were in formation, Hahnsbach snapped a salute to Valois and came to attention at the same time. "Company—te-HUN-shunn!"

The men snapped up straight.

"All present and accounted for, Sir." Hahnsbach said.

"Standing order number one," Valois said, still holding the gun in his hand. "Prepare for an attack."

Valois returned Sergeant Hahnsbach's salute. The big Sergeant spun around. "By the detail, standing order number one, prepare for an attack. Gun detail, *harch*! Water detail, *harch*! Supply detail, *harch*!" On and on, by two, three and four the men broke ranks and ran about the parade grounds carrying out their pre-assigned duties, until the ranks were down to a half-dozen. Hahnsbach turned to those remaining and directed them to take care of the bodies of Cook, Spivey and Daly.

Chuka, Trent, Jake and Henry lowered their guns and eased out of the confusion, stepping back out of the way. Valois had not moved. He stood, as if made of stone, not moving his head, unflinching, as the men bent to the task of moving the bodies. Jake and Henry stepped forward to help carry the dead Spivey and Daly.

Trent watched them, then looked at Valois and the dead men. He wiped his chin, looking up at Chuka. "Tough 'un, ain't he?"

"He's got sand," Chuka said slowly.

At that moment, Hahnsbach and a trooper came by carrying Cook's body. "He won't do no fightin' for a day or two," Trent observed.

Hahnsbach shook his head. "This one is dead—"

The two soldiers passed on with the body of Major Cook.

"Too bad," Chuka said, watching them pass.

"Why? After what he pulled?" Trent regarded Chuka.

"He was one more man against Hanu, wasn't he?" Chuka said.

"I never thought of that," Trent replied.

"I did," Chuka said coldly. He started to move away.

"Where you going?"

"First, to find a place where I can sit down peacefully, and second, to find something to drink."

"Ain't likely you'll find Valois willing to pass out likker at this time."

"There must be something on the place—maybe Sheppard or Evangeline have something."

"The drummer?" Trent asked. "And his wife?"

"Yeah," Chuka started to move away once more.

94

"Wait a minute, gunfighter," Trent said.

"What now?" Chuka asked, turning back.

"Well, I figure I owe you something for getting me outa that fix back yonder. I got a coupla bottles tucked away—"

"Lead on," Chuka said.

"You meet me in a few minutes over by the stables," Trent said. "I got me a good hiding place, and I don't want any of these dog soldiers finding it."

Chuka grinned and nodded. Trent limped off. When Chuka turned around, Valois was standing at his side, smiling, holding out his hand. "I want to thank you—for what you did a few minutes ago."

Chuka did not move. He leaned against the building and hung both thumbs in his gun-belt. He looked down at the outstretched hand, then slowly brought his eyes up, level with Valois' face. He made no move to shake hands.

The smile on Valois' lips faded. His jaw line tightened as his dropped his hand. "I see," he said, "your job is done."

"Done," Chuka replied. "You paid me, and I did what I was paid to do. Any arguments about that?"

"No arguments," Valois said. "And what happened a few minutes ago, when you stood up for me? How do you explain that, gunfighter?"

"What makes you think it was you I stood up for?" Chuka asked harshly.

"Then—"

"If those bastards had run out and left this place empty, what then?" Chuka asked, his voice hard and flat and even. "You were the only one to make them simmer down."

"Do you ever think about anything but yourself, gunfighter?" Valois asked, his lips curling with contempt.

"I wasn't thinking about you, Colonel," Chuka said.

"And what does your instinct for survival tell you to do now? Run? There is still time, you know."

Chuka looked toward the stables where Trent was motioning to him furtively. "I'll decide that, Colonel, when I think it's the right time."

"Will you take another job?" Valois asked, his voice icy and hard.

"Rider for help?" Chuka asked, meeting the younger man's steady gaze.

"To Fort Wallace."

"No."

"Same price."

"I said no."

"Double."

"Not for triple," Chuka said, watching Trent limp into the stables. "Excuse me, Colonel, I got to see somebody."

"Why not?" Valois asked, catching Chuka by the arm. Chuka looked down at the hand on his arm. The Colonel dropped his hand.

"The odds are against me," Chuka said. "Besides, I already got me a thousand dollars. I'd rather be alive and spend a thousand than die with four."

"And you never move unless the odds are in your favor, is that it?"

"Not when I got me a choice, Colonel," Chuka said. "Now if you will excuse me, Colonel—"

"How do you know the odds are against you?" Valois asked.

Chuka took a deep breath. "Do you trust Lou Trent?"

"What has he got to do with it?"

"Do you trust him?" Chuka insisted.

"Come'n," Chuka said wearily, "let him tell you."

Chuka stepped from the protection of the gallery and cut across the parade grounds. He did not look back to see if Valois was behind him. He walked into the stables. Chuka stood still a moment waiting for his eyes to grow accustomed to the light. "Lou—you in here?"

"Back here," Trent said from the depth of the stables. The old man limped into view. He held a full quart of whiskey in his right hand. "This here is government likker I stole from—" He saw Valois and stopped.

"Dammit, gunfighter, what'd you bring him along for?"

"He wants to ask you a question," Chuka said. He walked over to Trent, took the bottle, toasted him and took a tentative swallow.

Trent eyed Valois nervously.

"What are the chances of getting a man through to Wallace, Trent?" Valois asked.

Trent licked his lips, seeing Chuka take a deep swallow. "Uh—uh—what'd you say, Colonel?"

"I want you to ride to Fort Wallace."

Trent did not reply. He watched Chuka take a deep drink, his eyes hanging on the gurgling whiskey. "Good, ain't it?" Trent said throatily.

Chuka lowered the bottle and handed it to the old scout. "Good," he gasped, his face turning red.

Valois waited impatiently. Trent wet his lips. "Well, here's to you gunfighter, fer what you did back yonder. You sure looked good to me, coming up the side of that hill with that shooter of yourn throwing lead." Trent raised the bottle.

"Mr. Trent!" Valois would not be ignored any longer. "I want you to ride to Fort Wallace at once."

Trent lowered the bottle. He looked at Chuka, then at the bottle. He sighed and twisted his shoulder in resignation. "Won't do no good," he said finally.

"Is that Lou Trent, or the bottle, talking?" Valois asked sarcastically.

"I ain't even took a drink yet," Trent said.

"Are you refusing to ride to Fort Wallace?"

"You wanta kill me?" Trent asked.

"Are you saying there's no chance of your getting through?" Valois demanded.

"About as much chance as a she-bear against a Ballard fifty!" Trent said, and quickly brought the bottle to his lips, taking a long drink. When he eased off, he stared at Valois. "Any man sent outside this Fort is a dead'un, Colonel."

Valois looked at Chuka, who shrugged. "I'm ordering you, Mr. Trent, to saddle up at once and ride to Fort Wallace."

Trent looked at Chuka, who grinned at him. "I'll take care of your whiskey for you, Lou," Chuka said.

"Colonel—" Trent tried one last appeal on Valois.

"Report to my office. I'll have the dispatch ready by the time you're saddled up." Valois turned and started for the door. He had gained the entrance when a call came from the high north tower.

"They're coming—they're coming. Attack! Attack!"

Valois ran from the door. From somewhere within the walls, a bugler began sounding the *Charge!*

Trent and Chuka walked slowly to the door and watched the running men as they took up their positions around the Fort. Valois had climbed to the north tower and was shouting orders. Jake and Henry appeared around the corner of the stables, their eyes untroubled. Chuka took the bottle and drank from it, then handed it back to Trent, who took a drink. The bottle was passed to Jake and Henry. "This would be Hanu's probe," Chuka said.

"Yeah," Trent replied. All four men listened as the pounding of horses' hooves, carrying the lead riders, approached the Fort. A rifle cracked—then another—then several.

"Hold your fire—hold your fire!" Valois shouted. "Wait for the order—pass the word—Sergeant Hahnsbach! Pass the word!"

Sergeant Hahnsbach's bull-throated roar repeated the order. The random nervous fire stopped. The sound of the hooves became louder. Trent cocked his head. "Sounds like about thirty of them," he said.

"More like fifty," Chuka replied.

Jake took a drink from the bottle, hesitated, then nodded. "Forty for sure, huh, Henry?"

"Forty," Henry said and took a drink. The shooting started again, and the bottle made another round. A door opened on the far side of the parade grounds and Señora Veronica Klietz stepped into view. She looked about, watching the activity. Her eyes stopped on the four men standing quietly at the entrance to the stables, drinking and not looking in the least concerned with the fury of the fight going on around them. She was startled for a moment; then turned and looked up at the north tower where Valois was firing, shouting and commanding. She frowned and turned back to the four men, her frown turning into a smile. Chuka looked up and saw her, tipped his hat and nodded. Veronica Klietz barely nodded her head and stepped back inside the door, closing it.

Nearly three dozen guns, spread along the top of the Fort's walls, fired steadily. The hooves of the horses outside the Fort were heavy and made the earth shake where the four men stood in the weak, fading November sun.

The bottle made the rounds again. "Forty for sure," Trent said. "That sun feels damn good, don't it?" He said happily. Everyone agreed.

"This whiskey of yours feels better, though," Henry said.

Jake was watching the fighting on the walls, his eyes moving from one gun to another. He turned now, his eyes bright. "Let's go up and watch how these soldiers making out, Henry."

"All right," Henry said slowly. He took another quick drink, and, with Jake, walked towards the nearest ladder that lead to the catwalk around the walls.

Trent took a long swallow from the bottle. "I got me a coupla more bottles like that," he said shaking his shoulders happily.

"You're lucky old Hanu sent in his probe when he did," Chuka said.

"Don't I know it," Trent answered.

Both men looked up at the high north tower where Valois was firing rapidly, wing shooting with his pistol.

"Whew! I'm getting tired and sleepy," Trent said.

"I feel fine," Chuka said. The bottle passed between them again. Both men were watching the young Colonel.

"Two days?" Chuka asked easily.

"I figure two days," Trent said. "If we do pretty good tomorrow and hang on the next day—that'll do it."

"We'll get it in the morning—first thing," Chuka said. "All of 'em."

"Oh, they'll all come tomorrow," Trent agreed, his tongue getting thick. "First they'll send in about a third from the west—then just about time we get set for that bunch, the main force will come up outa the sun."

"Ain't this hell?" Chuka said amiably, grinning foolishly, feeling the whiskey burn in his stomach.

"I tol' him—then las' night when I slipped out, I found out right away I been right all summer about Hanu—and I started out for Wallace."

"But you weren't fast enough."

"Fast as anything you'll see, you young whelp!" Trent said with drunken belligerence. "They was just too many of them waiting for me."

"Why ain't there been no telegraph put into Clendennon?" Chuka asked.

"Been put in, an' been put in, an' been put in. I don't know how many times. Always getting tore down by some raggedy-tailed Injun. Spent half the time las' year scoutin' for patrols out puttin' the wire back up. Been down a coupla weeks now—miles of it."

The fighting on the walls raged on, steady and intense.

"You think they hittin' anything?" Trent asked.

"Some—horses mostly, sounds like to me."

"I figured that too," Trent replied. They passed the bottle between them one more time. There was one gulp's worth left in the bottom. Chuka politely offered it to Trent.

"Naw, go on, kill it, gunfighter. I'm going to sleep now." The old scout turned away from the furious fighting going on around them and limped to the back of the stables.

Chuka watched as a soldier, holding his shoulder and bleeding badly, was helped down from the walls and carried over to the officers' mess where Helena, Eve and Veronica Klietz opened the door to receive the wounded man.

Chuka killed the bottle and tossed it to one side. Grinning foolishly, he stepped into the stables.

He found a dry stall, took the horse by the lead and doubled the animal up with the one in the next stall. He sat down in a pile of fresh hay and removed his .44. Whistling softly to himself, he began to take apart the gun and clean it. Chuka stopped once to remove his boots, then continued cleaning the pistol.

The sun went down and the firing stopped. The Indians' shouting and the pounding of their horses' hooves outside the walls of Clendennon were gone by the time Chuka had finished cleaning both his .44 and his carbine. He eased back in the hay, pushed his hat over his eyes and was just about to drop off to sleep, listening to the snoring of Trent further back in the stables, when he heard someone enter. Chuka eased up the brim of his hat an inch and saw Valois standing before him.

Valois' face was grim, streaked, his eyes bloodshot. "Where's Trent?"

"He fought himself clean out, Colonel," Chuka lied. He rolled over and leaned on one elbow. "He had a hard time last night. He's

100

an old man. Soon as they beat it, both of us came down here to get as much rest as we could."

"Where were you? I saw Watkins and Crowford, but I didn't see you."

"Well—both of us fought from the sally port, Colonel," Chuka said. Then seeing Valois' eyes narrow, added quickly. "Ground level."

"Oh."

"Something on your mind, Colonel?"

"Oh, no, nothing in particular," Valois replied. "But I guess you and Lou were right. To have sent a man out—would have meant his death."

"Yeah—it sure as hell would have."

There followed a moment of silence. Chuka watched the younger man stir restlessly. "How'd we do out there?" Chuka asked.

"Not too well. The men weren't taking their time."

"They'd damn sure better take their time tomorrow," Chuka said.

"Do you always react so—indifferently to a crisis?" Valois asked.

Chuka sat up. He studied Valois intently for a moment. "Sit down, Colonel. You look tired."

"Yes, I am tired." Valois rested his back against one of the stalls and slipped down to a sitting position.

Chuka rolled and lit a cigarette, puffed it several times. "This the first time, Colonel'?" He asked.

"First time for what?"

"Killing a man in cold blood."

Valois snapped his head around, his jaws working. He looked into Chuka's eyes. "You know why I'm here, don't you?"

"Probably."

"Yes," Valois said slowly, "the first time." He looked at his hands, making fists out of them. "One with my fists and one with a gun."

"Fists don't count," Chuka said. "Lucky blow, probably. Hit him just right. It ain't easy to kill a man with your fists. It's harder than most people think."

"And there is the heat of battle—"

"That too," Chuka agreed.

"But Spivey."

"Was that his name?"

"Theodore Spivey. I had to do it."

"Sure you did," Chuka said. "And you timed it just right. A little more mouth from that one, and they would have swarmed over you like bees out of a hive."

"Ever stop to think where we all would be if there weren't any guns?"

"We'd fight with sticks—or stones."

"Or fists."

"Or fists," Chuka agreed.

Valois stirred himself and regarded Chuka. "I shouldn't be bothering you. I wonder what you must think of me after this morning in the office."

"You didn't hurt me, Colonel," Chuka said. "But you did make one mistake."

"What?"

"You should have let me and Jake and Henry take the women out when we had a chance."

"It was stupid of me to think—" Valois started.

"Think what? That I was using it as an excuse to run?"

Valois hesitated. He nodded finally.

"Hell, man, you didn't have to believe me. Didn't Jake or Henry say the same thing to you?"

"You made me so mad," Valois said.

Chuka said nothing.

"What did you and Sergeant Hahnsbach fight about?"

"Nothing in particular. Just letting off steam."

"That's what he said, in so many words."

"Good man, Hahnsbach. He moved right in and took over after you drilled that big mouth. You coulda lost it then, if it hadn't been for him."

"I recognize that."

"One thing has been bothering me, Colonel."

"What?"

"You being so young and the Army putting you in charge of a bunch of hard tails like you got here."

Valois turned and looked Chuka in the eye. "You are a very perceptive man. Chuka," he said slowly. "It was the wrong job to give me."

"Oh?"

"Handling men—men who will take an order and carry it out, is not the same as trying to make over a—" he glanced at Chuka, "bunch of hard tails."

"Think the Army slipped up?"

"They go by the record. It's the only real measure they have. What is a man's record?"

"You must have a damn good one to be a colonel at your age."

"I have one of the finest records in the Army, Chuka," Valois said with a shrug. "But it wasn't enough to—give me the wisdom I should have had today."

"Don't cry over spilled milk, Colonel."

"Two things. The women should have been sneaked out, and I should have spotted Spivey. I know his record—what there was of it until he got here. But since he's been here, he's been the model soldier—by the record."

"Well," Chuka drawled, "you caught up with him in the end. That's what counts."

"I had the strangest feeling after I killed him, Chuka. One moment he had been standing before me, jeering in my face; and the next moment he was a lifeless, dead carcass at my feet."

"There'll be a lot more before you get out of this one, Colonel. Death will stink to high heaven before it's over."

"You sound—confident—away from it—as if it had nothing whatsoever to do with you."

"That so?" Chuka looked at him.

"Do you think you will survive, then?"

"I believe that I will see it through, yes," Chuka said slowly.

"Why the confidence? You've painted yourself to be a coldly realistic man, who checks both sides before he makes a move, and finally, insists that the odds be in his favor. And now you show me a side—"

"Colonel," Chuka said slowly, "you killed a man today. And you got a strange feeling, as you described it, seeing him alive one minute and dead the next."

"Yes."

"Think back now, to that moment when you were facing the soldiers. What were you thinking?"

"Why—I'm not sure."

"Well, did you doubt that you would succeed?"

"I can't truthfully say," Valois replied.

"Were you scared?"

"Yes—in the beginning. Especially when Spivey started talking against me."

"Do you think now, looking back on it, that you could have ever let them walk over you without your doing something to stop them?"

"No I wouldn't have just stood there."

"Then you have—or you had—a little of what I feel at the moment. It ain't confidence. It's—training. You in your way, me in mine. You killed one man. I've gunned down quite a few. The feeling grows stronger each time. And after each time, Colonel, you get so you can see how the thing repeats itself over and over and over. A man is faced with something that will take his life away from him—a thing so scary he *can't* think about it—at the moment. But with experience, Colonel, you can look back over the way things happened, and you can see how they probably will happen that way again. Training and ability will kind of take over and see you through."

Chuka paused and rolled another cigarette. "First time out for me, I thought sure I was going to die, right then and there. But I didn't. Something in me kept me from thinking I was really going to die."

"If it isn't confidence, then what is it? Valois asked.

"I don't know," Chuka replied slowly. "But I've thought about it a long time. Many times. With every man I've faced, I think back about that man, and I *know* that if it had to be done again, just the same way all over again, I would walk away and he would be dead."

"The difference between being a winner and a loser," Valois said.

"Maybe. I can't put a name to it for you."

"But as of now, you truly believe that you will survive?"

"I couldn't any more tell you *how*, or under what conditions, or when I'll be sprung outa this situation; but I believe it, Colonel; I believe it. But I don't think about it."

"And I," Valois said, "I cannot see how I will walk away from it."

"Maybe you're one of those men I faced in the past; and if it had to be done over again, it would be the same. Maybe you're one of them. But I want to tell you this. You looked pretty damn good out there today."

"Thank you," Valois said after a long pause. He stood and looked down at Chuka. "Could you call it—attitude?"

"You mean the way you look at something?"

Valois nodded.

"It might be that," Chuka said. "It might be. I sure as hell know it isn't confidence—our courage—or being brave."

"No—it isn't any of those things. It must be attitude."

"Well," Valois took a deep breath. "I'd better go set the watch."

"Yeah," Chuka said.

"Good night, gunfighter."

"Good night, Colonel."

Valois looked down once more and stared at the big man with the guns cleaned and ready, then turned and walked from the stables.

Chuka did not sleep right away. He had never talked about his life before, not in this way. He rolled the word attitude over in his mind. He ranged back over his years in the saddle, and the towns, and the cow camps and the gunplay. He looked at each man again, as he had once, in the rain, the snow, the heat—there had been many places, and in that moment, he was staring at all of them. They were all alike—he had been just the same; except for that first time, standing there, sure, rock hard, deadly—knowing that he was going to put the other man down.

Attitude. A way of looking at something—things—life, even death.

In the deep silence of the stables, Chuka slept, finally, soundly.

Chapter Eight

SIX men at Fort Clendennon on the 18th of November awoke at five o'clock in the morning. They did so independently of each other, without the benefit of having someone call to wake them. They emerged from their sleeping places, two from the hayloft, two from the horse stalls, two from the passenger cab of the stagecoach, and walked across the hard ground, their boots crunching on the frost, and gathered in the kitchen within five minutes of each other. Six men, their heads tucked into the collars of their coats, chins bent downward against the cold, their hands deep in their pockets—just dark figures on a dark morning, getting a jump on the daylight, gathering in the kitchen near the stove, puffy-faced from their recent hard sleep—all within themselves.

Chuka was the first to arrive. He stoked the fire in the stove and set about making a pot of coffee. Trent came next, looking up at Chuka, a light of surprise in his eyes. Then, after a grunt, to which Chuka did not respond, he moved over to the stove and warmed his hands. Jake Crowford came in next, carrying two Winchester carbines, a short-barreled .44-40 Colt and a Liverwright shotgun. Jake also carried a leather pouch filled with shells. He looked at Chuka and Trent, nodded briefly, then went to the far side of the stove and began to work on the guns. Baldwin and Howard came in together, their faces red, carrying their guns. Baldwin carried a Henry rifle, the squared stock and magazine familiar to all of them; Howard had a Winchester '73 rifle with a full twenty-seven inch barrel, as well as a .45 Colt. Henry Watkins was the last to come in, a frown on his face. He looked around anxiously, then saw that Crowford had the guns and relaxed. He was the only one of the six to speak. "Morning," he mumbled, and shoved past Baldwin and Howard to Jake's side. He picked up one of the carbines, and without a word, began stripping it down.

Trent, his shakes almost gone, which came from a combination of age, hangover and the cold, was warmed enough to settle down. He picked up an old Henry carbine, looked at the gun distrustfully, shook his head and began taking it down. "Had me one of them good Winchester seventy-three rifles—no carbine—but I lost it back yonder," the old man said to no one in general.

A dog howled in the distance. Trent looked up. The other men paused and looked at Trent. He waited, then nodded. They all knew then that it was a real dog, probably one that had followed Hanu's group. The dog was a favorite of one of the bucks; otherwise it would have stayed back in camp with the women and children.

When the coffee began to boil, Chuka pulled the pot to the side of the stove. The others looked up. Trent frowned and looked pointedly at the pot. Chuka sighed and shoved the pot back onto the stove to boil some more.

Chuka walked across the kitchen to the half door. In the silence of the room, his Texas spurs, two-inch sunbursts, tinkled like bells. He stooped over, unbuckled the straps and threw the spurs to one side. Then he stood up and studied the skyline that was broken by the log pole pikes on the walls of the Fort. The sky was still black, but there was a darker, less penetrable black along the base of the walls. Though he could not make out the sentries on the north and west towers, he knew they were there, pacing their posts; now and then he could hear their even, steady steps, comforting, reassuring.

Trent had stopped his delicate work over the firing mechanism and was watching Jake. "That's mighty interesting," he said, "but what in hell are you doing?"

Jake Crowford looked up, surprised that Trent was speaking to him. "Oh—nothin'," Jake said.

Henry, wiping down his carbine, answered Trent. "They ain't got enough punch for Jake," he said, indicating the shells, a mound of black powder and leads neatly arranged on a table before the tall thin man.

"That's a Winny seventy-three, ain't it?" Trent asked, indicating the carbine at Jake's side.

"Yeah," Jake said. "This 'un and Henry's are one in a thousand."

Baldwin and Howard looked up. Baldwin spoke. "One in one thousand," he said with deep appreciation. "One hundred dollars each." He turned to Trent. "Winchester drummer tried to sell me one. They made up just one thousand of 'em, and sold 'em for one hundred dollars each. Mighty superior weapon."

"Is that so?" Trent said. "Here, mind if I take a look."

Jake passed the gun to Trent, who handled it with respect.

Chuka came over to look at the weapon, taking it from Trent, hefting it, judging its weight, and nodded, giving the gun his approval.

Trent looked back at Jake, who was busy working over the shells, powder and leads. "And you making your own fittin's for it?"

"Not exactly," Jake said slowly. "All the seventy-threes, and after, are chambered for the forty-four-forty, so a feller don't have to buy one shell for his hand gun and another for his rifle. But I always did like a little more to my rifle shooting."

"What do you use?" Chuka asked with interest.

"I up it from forty grains of black powder to fifty, and put in a two-fifty-five grain lead."

Chuka's professional interest was peaked. "Doesn't this throw the lead up—when you back it with that much power?"

"It'll rise about two inches in thirty yards," Jake said.

"Wouldn't you want that much kick in a rifle rather than a carbine?" Trent asked.

"Don't like rifles," Jake replied. "I guess it was what you was raised with. Paw, back in Kansas, had a Sharps fifty-two carbine that came with a twenty-two-inch barrel. Paw never did like a long gun, and had three inches taken off it. It had a hell of a wallop." Jake grinned at them. "I got used to short sights and a lot of kick as a young'un. "

Trent nodded. "Now there was this feller down south of the Traces had an old Ballard fifty, bluffer gun. He did like you. Made it up. Lead and all." Trent looked at his own Henry, his face a little disgusted. "I sure hated to lose that good Winchester to them heathen Injuns out yonder," he sighed, "but this Henry'll do me."

When the coffee was ready, they all stopped their work on the guns, putting four and five teaspoons of sugar in their cups, sipping at the hot, sticky brew and smoking, enjoying the luxury of the warm kitchen, the coffee and the talk.

The talk was about guns. It would probably be about guns any time six men found themselves together, in a companionable mood.

"That Spencer now—that was a good rifle," Howard said.

"It was, it was," Baldwin agreed. "And in the hands of an Apache, he could just about shoot the devil in the tail if he showed it."

"And that big gun Sharps put out. You know the one I mean?" Henry Watkins asked, looking around at them. "Trent, you old enough—"

"You mean that damn cannon—?"

"That's the one. It was bigger'n a Ballard fifty."

"Bigger'n anything," the old scout said. "Hell, that thing was fifty—about one-sixty, seventy, and up to seven hundred grain lead!"

"Shoot good, huh?" Howard asked.

"Hell, that thing would shoot across the Mississippi and hit a Memphis gambler before he could pull that extra ace," Trent said.

"Fine gun," Henry said. "Fine gun."

"It was, it surely was," Trent agreed. "But I got to say this, the weapons we got now, refined and all as they are, they still ain't got the straight accuracy we used to get in the mountain days."

"You had longer barrels," Jake said with a sly dig. "And besides, by the time the load would get out'n the end, you could count your fingers and toes."

Everyone chuckled. "Well, that may be so; but a steady man could take 'em down, I tell you."

"You got anything against this Colt six-gun?" Chuka asked, patting the weapon. The others quietened as Chuka hauled out the big black-handled .44 and handed it over to Trent.

Trent eased forward and hefted the gun. "Man—that's a gun—*that's* a gun."

Chuka's weapon was passed around, and they all admired it.

"I go along with Jake on the chambering," Chuka said. "I wouldn't want to have to haul around two shells—"

"Well," Baldwin asked easily, "what'd you tote before that Frontier .44 came out?"

"I had the .45," Chuka said. "Before that, I had a honey of a gun."

They all waited.

"Dragoon Colt." Chuka said.

The men in the room sighed and rocked back, nodding in agreement.

"Dragoons—"

"It *was* a honey of a gun—"

"Blow you clean through—"

"Well, it was chambered right for the weight and—"

"I had a Spencer for a long time," Howard said. "Fine gun. Then I got me the Winchester. Only thing wrong with that Indian-model Spencer was, the lever action would jam."

Chuka nodded from the stove where he was pouring himself another cup of coffee. "And they would do it in the damndest places."

"You sound like you *know*," Trent said, winking at the others.

"I was in a situation," Chuka said, dead pan, his voice mild.

"And it jammed?" Trent asked.

"It did."

"And you did what?"

Chuka, still dead pan, looked at Trent. "Why, I took his gun," he paused and looked away, "After I got to him."

They burst into laughter.

"Then I discovered the only reason I got to him was because *he* had a Spencer that jammed —"

The men roared with laughter.

"Wasn't it a Spencer they had down to the Washita fight?" Henry asked Baldwin.

"Yeah," the stageman said dourly. "It worked fine there. On the wimmen and kids too —"

"Yeah," Trent said bitterly.

The all thought about the slaughter of the Cheyenne, and though they themselves were waiting for the Arapaho to attack, they still could not abide the murder of every living soul at the Cheyenne camp eight years before.

"Well, I don't like Injuns with rifles in their hands; but I ain't saying I cried when I heard that big-mouthed Custer got his'n."

No one said anything; but each man agreed, at least partially, with Trent.

In the silence that followed the mention of Custer, the six men settled within themselves; they were fully awake now. Dan Howard took out a daguerreotype of his wife and studied it in the faint light from the one lamp; Baldwin pulled one foot up to the edge of his chair and began to scrape the mud from his boot heel; Jake continued remaking his extra-powered shells for his carbine and Henry finished cleaning his own gun. Trent pulled out a Bowie knife and began to hone it; Chuka paced carrying one of the spurs, snapping the wheel with his finger.

110

Suddenly Chuka stopped and looked at Trent. "What time?" He asked. His voice was harsh in the silence.

"About half-hour before sunup, we should be ready," Trent said and made another pass on the stone with the knife blade. He stopped and though a moment. "They might be working in now, with fire bundles."

Jake looked up and nodded. "They did that once, down to Claryway. The Apaches."

Henry nodded. "That's right. Me and Jake were driving beeves up from deep Texas. They jumped us at this place and we high-tailed it to the Fort. Snuck up in the dark that night with fire bundles. Then set up strong bows and hit 'em dead center with flame arrows."

"Burnt us right to the ground," Jake said.

"I heard about Claryway," Trent said, nodding his head. "You did good."

"Well," Henry said, a little awkwardly, "we was lucky we had some real sweet, sugar guns with us, a bunch about like this one—off the Pecos. Only there wasn't no four or five hundred."

Chuka was thoughtful and stopped his pacing. "We need a good man sitting up in that high tower, using all his know-how with a gun—and when first light comes, we might get a few—"

"That's be Jake," Henry said at once. "He's all right—"

"Jake?" Trent said.

"Why sure," Jake said. He stuffed the last of his shells into his pockets, picked up the carbine and loaded it. He slipped his stumpy-barreled .45 into his holster and picked up the Liverwright shotgun. He paused, looked at the shotgun, and tossed it to Henry. "Bring this up to me later. Might get lost—or something—" he finished quietly. Jake stepped up to the stove, poured a second cup of coffee, which he took with him, and passed through the door.

When he was gone, Henry pronounced the verdict, "He'll hit something now and then."

"Where are you going to sit, gunfighter?" Trent asked.

"I like ground shooting," Chuka said. "Feet have been on the ground most of the time I had to shoot. My judgment would be better there."

"Makes sense," Trent said, honing the knife.

Chuka paced the length of the kitchen several times, and then at the end of the room, instead of turning, went through the doorway.

"Saved my bacon," Trent said, with a jerk of his head after Chuka, without looking at Baldwin, Howard, or Henry.

"I never could cotton to a gunslick," Baldwin said, "but I heard about this 'un long before he came to my town of Trinidad."

Henry spoke slowly, but he wanted his thoughts known. "He's my friend," he said matter-of-factly. There would be no loose talk behind Chuka's back now, or Henry would stand up for him.

Trent came in quickly. "Hoss," he said quietly to Henry, "I'm on his side. I said he saved my bacon."

Henry said nothing.

Trent turned to Baldwin. "Do anything in your town?" He asked.

"We had a little situation," Baldwin said soberly. "The man never did me no harm, mind; but there was plenty that he pushed around. Man name of Holly. Mark Holly. The gunslick hired on opposite Holly."

"It musta been good for his side, 'cause he's still walking. How's this here Holly?" Trent asked.

"Dead—with a coupla more thrown in for good measure."

"Well, he saved my bacon and I'm owin' to him," Trent said.

"I don't cotton to gunslicks," Baldwin said again. "But this 'un, he'll do."

"You're damn right he'll do," Henry said.

Chuka returned loaded down with six canteens, one for each man, filled and capped. He handed them over. "This one is Jake's, isn't it?"

"I'll see he gets it," Henry said. "Hey, gunfighter," Trent said. "Yeah?"

"Can you move that thing?" Trent asked, nodding to the big .44.

"Before you finish blinking your eye," Chuka replied.

"Show me," Trent said, at once ceasing to hone the knife and leaning forward. The others stopped and stared.

And then he was shown. The big man had the gun in his hand and the barrel in Trent's face, the hammer thumbed back, all in a fraction of a second.

"Better'n you used to be," Trent said in the knowing way of an old man being coy.

112

"When did you see me?" Chuka demanded.

"Dodge City—long time ago." Trent looked at the others. "Long time ago; but he's lots better now." He nodded wisely.

"I've had more experience," Chuka said matter-of-factly.

"There was a sharp, high whine—the powerful whine of a rifle shot. The sound broke the morning stillness like a thunderclap. The men looked at each other; then they all looked at Henry.

"Jake," Henry said, confirming their unasked question.

"He musta seen something," Trent said, resuming his honing.

"Well, if he saw something, he hit whatever he saw—man, beastie, fowl in the air. If Jake saw it, and shot at it—he hit."

The shot woke Clendennon. Seconds after the overloaded carbine had fired, the air was split with the hoarse voices of men cursing, roused from their sleep, lunging around in the dark.

The friendly, comfortable atmosphere among the five men was broken by the half-dressed figure and excited face of Hahnsbach. He stared at the men. "What is it? They coming?"

"Naw, hell, they ain't coming yit," Trent said. "Go back to bed, Sarge. I'll wake you in time," the old man added sarcastically.

The sergeant turned from the door and rushed away.

The carbine on the high tower cracked again.

Henry stood up. "Might as well go on up. Can't let Jake have it all. Of course I gotta wait for daylight. I ain't no puma cat like Jake who can see anything in the dark."

The leathery faced man got up slowly, took his guns, canteen and the Liverwright, and gingerly handling a mug of coffee, shuffled from the kitchen.

Baldwin and Howard stood, stretched and left the kitchen without a word—partners, moving along with each other, without speaking, yet knowing after years of life together just exactly what the other one would do. Trent watched them go.

"Well, gunfighter, it's here; and that ain't no lie." He stretched. "Do good out there today. I wouldn' tell the Colonel, but if we can give 'em hell their first two tries, without losing on our side, we got a small chance." He picked up the ancient Henry rifle, looked at it with distaste and shuffled to the door. Trent looked back at Chuka. "I got another bottle or two. Don't forget now. Tonight at the stables."

Chuka waved, not moving his arm, just bending his wrist, palm down, and made the typical Indian gesture that Trent and the others were getting used to. "You wait for me, now, heah?" Chuka said.

Trent limped out into the darkness.

Chuka stood a moment and stared at the tiny hole in the top of the stove and the red coals inside the firebox. He sipped the coffee.

Sugar guns—the phrase stuck in his mind.

And then suddenly, without knowing why, but not resisting it, he stared at the tiny hole and the red coals inside and, as if hypnotized, was instantly in deep thought.

—*before you can finish blinking your eye*—

A mighty big boast, sugar gun.

Yet, it was absolutely accurate. It was more than accurate. He was faster than the blink of a man's eyes.

"Chuka," he said aloud.

Chuka—beef and beans—beef and sourdough—a stripling from the Texas flats, a deep, hot, level, angry land where his parents had worked themselves lean to hold a place, deep in the southwest country—and had failed. They died decent, in bed, worked out, before he was a full-grown man.

A boy fifteen, already his full height, but so skinny the range boss didn't think he would stand the gaff in the saddle, and put him on the chuck wagon; and he became Chuka.

—Gimme coffee, Chuka—

—More o' them damn beans, dammit, Chuka—

—Yew git up at four and start the fire, and measure the flour for the baking batch—

In the rain and sleet and cold. Chuka. The helper that built the fire and collected the firewood when they were in wood country, or took the wagon out and loaded it up and hauled it back, when they were not. Chuka. The skinny boy who never spoke and worked like a horse, sixteen and eighteen hours a day—twenty when it rained—and hustled the grub when they came in, angry mean, sweaty and woman hungry, pinched for the need, tasting the whiskey in the trail towns before they came within riding distance—

Chuka. The boy who took all the jokes and never talked back, who understood them, and was one of them. And who knew that except for the very few, the dog-wolves that came along in every range camp, they meant no harm.

Chuka. No different from any of them. Growing up like a man should on the Texas flats, growing hard, and tasting cruelty, fighting it when it was wise, taking it when it was take it or be killed.

Chuka. Boy among the men. Learning the grooves of life in that part of the country. Mr. Prince Bradford had said he would put him in the saddle the following year.

That winter the Mexican Pistolero came jangling into the bunk-house, a drifter, a man who would quit when the spring roundup came and real work was to be done.

Chuka saw the guns, heard the spurs, watched the hard cases in the bunkhouse give him the wide-open, and it was done, then and there.

The Pistolero taught Chuka about the guns. He learned what the gun was supposed to do and the whole philosophy behind the gun's true meaning and purpose. He knew it from the inside out, learned about the guns as people learn by experience in life.

Guns fascinated him, awed him. They sent shivers of revulsion through him. He had dreams about guns—and nightmares.

A gun did not have to be fired to prove its point. A gun was a threat. Empty, it still carried the message.

That spring Chuka used a gun for the first time. A man went down with a bullet in his heart, dead before he hit the ground, sorry, oh so sorry, an instant before he died, that he had cuffed the Chuka—boy for not giving him his coffee fast enough.

Mr. Prince Bradford fired him on the spot.

He was committed from that moment on.

—before you can finish blinking your eye—

"If you draw a line," Chuka had once said to a U.S. Marshal that had ordered him out of town after a gunfight," and you stand on your side of the line, and I stand on mine, that line, and nothing else, separates us, or me, from any other man that carries a gun. Just a line. On your side, it's all good; on mine, it's all bad."

But the gun was not always used against men. Once he used it when he had wrenched his back after his horse stumbled, fell and rolled on him, a brown bear went for the horse. The horse ran; the bear ran. The bear was winning the race. From a half-sitting position, the pain was so intense he could hardly raise his arm, Chuka had fired six times, the recoil searing him with pain. It had taken six bullets to stop the bear and save the horse. Without the horse, Chuka would have died where he lay. Only a gunman could have done it.

Speed and accuracy.

Another time Chuka used the gun when he crawled into a hole in the Nevada mountains to escape from a storm. Luckily he saw the head of the rattler coiled, ready to strike. He drew and got him before the snake could strike—and then in the flash of the first shot, saw the head of a second on his right—and got him.

Only a gunslick, whose hand was trained to move with speed and accuracy and to shoot without thinking, only the gunfighter would have been able to get out of the hole in the Nevada mountains alive.

The Mexican pistolero had died decently, with a fat woman to cry over him and four fine boys to grow up thinking kindly of their father. The pistolero had not only shown the Chuka-boy the gun, its use, its handling, the tricks, the ways, he also had given Chuka the ideas that must accompany the gun—ideas that the pistolero had learned from his father who had ridden with Santa Anna, one of those who survived Houston's slaughter of the Mexicans at San Jacinto.

A gun is not God. A gun is nothing until it is picked up and used by another man. Not a dog, or a steer, but a man. Another man may have a gun. So you must out-think him. Out-thinking the other man must always add up to your having the advantage. Never give the advantage to the other fellow.

A time in Lincoln County.

His gun was empty. To have admitted it would have meant death. He refused to fight. He allowed himself to be pistol-whipped; but he did not draw. He still wore the scars from that beating on his head with the barrel of a hand gun; the gun-sight had cut deep gashes in his head. But Chuka did not fight. He allowed himself to be called yellow. To draw would have been death.

In six weeks when Chuka was well enough to walk, he found the man. He had been the one Lou Trent saw in Dodge City.

Chuka's real name ceased to mean anything.

He became Chuka.

Once in Montana country, that land where there was all the distance for the eye to travel and then some: "Chuka—iss not a naime—Chuka sunds lak somethang iss to eat—"

"The name is Chuka, Half Breed."

"Chuka - iss somethan' a man vomits afta drink too much—you goin to draw dat gun, Chuka man?"

"When I pull a gun, I kill a man."

"Keel me, Chuka-vomit—!"

Where had such speed come from? Half Breed had, by far, the fastest draw he had ever seen. Three things had ripped through Chuka, and at the same time, he had seen Half Breed fall backwards into the hog pen—three things and that feeling of dizziness when Chuka saw his own blood spewing from three places. The heat he felt at that moment had been the heat of his life.

But Half Breed was dead.

"Señor—"

Chuka heard something.

"Señor!"

He stared at the hole in the stove, saw Half Breed.

"Señor Chuka?" The voice was tentative, a little afraid.

Chuka turned around. Helena Chavez stood in the doorway.

He stared, seeing her, not comprehending her presence. The last thought, and Half Breed's words, still rang in his brain.

When you pulled a gun, you killed a man.

It was time he was through with it—sugar gun—

Chapter Nine

CHUKA did not move or speak for a moment. He could only stare at her. "Ma'am?" He said finally. "Can I help you?" He tipped his hat.

"We need water, Señor Chuka, for the wounded man. Hot water."

"Yes ma'am. I'll see that you get hot water right away."

"Thank you." Helena Chavez started to withdraw.

"Oh, ma'am— "

"Yes?"

"There's hot coffee. And if you don't mind my saying so, you look like you could use a cup. Either that or some sleep."

She hesitated. Chuka moved quickly, taking the pot and reaching for a mug. "Here— it's all ready."

Again she hesitated, looked at him. Chuka's face softened. He tried to smile. "It's all right, Miss Chavez."

She returned his smile and slowly came forward.

"Yes, I would like coffee. The others could use some as well."

"I'll put on another pot and get it right over there with the hot water. Here, sit down."

"Thank you."

Helena sat down, her back straight, her lips pressed tightly together. She did not touch the coffee Chuka put before her. He pumped water into a huge pot and put it on the stove, stoked the fire, putting on more wood, and then set about preparing a second pot of coffee. When he turned back, she had not moved.

He stepped forward and picked up the mug of coffee before her. "The coffee, ma'am," he said gently.

She looked up startled, as if surprised to see him, then lowered her eyes. "Thank you."

Chuka stepped back, leaned against the wall and looked at her. "If you're worried about the fight, ma'am—"

She looked up at him. "Como?"

"Is something bothering you, ma'am? If it's the fight coming up, it won't be easy; but we're in a pretty good position."

118

"The fight, si. What does it matter?"

"What does what matter, ma'am?"

"I am sorry, Senior Chuka." She stood quickly and started for the door. "Thank you for the coffee—the others will appreciate it, Señora Sheppard is very tired."

Chuka moved toward her. "Ma'am, mind if I ask you a personal question?"

She stared up a moment. "I must hurry—"

"Señora Klietz said yesterday morning you two were going back to Trinidad and not on to the east."

"Please Senior—"

"I don't want to be nosy; but if there is anything I can do to help."

She stared at the big man. Her eyes studied his face.

"Help? Not even you—or this—" She touched the butt of the big .44 with her fingers.

"But both me and the gun, ma'am."

"No."

"Why don't you tell me?"

"There is very little to tell, Senior; and nothing to be done. Perhaps this is the best way after all—then no one will ever know."

"Know what? What is best after all?" Chuka asked.

"To die here at this place," Helena Chavez said. She shivered.

"Know what, ma'am?" Chuka insisted gently. "It must be pretty terrible to make a beautiful woman like you want to die."

"I must go." Helena Chavez threw a startled look at Chuka, turned and vanished into the darkness. Chuka moved after her, stopping at the door. She did not turn around as she hurried across the frozen ground toward the lighted window of the officers' mess.

The cooks came in, bustling with cold, brushed past Chuka and stood before the stove.

"What's this water for?" A cook asked.

"Take that over to the hospital when it gets hot," Chuka said absently, still looking at the lighted window in the officers' mess. "And the coffee—"

"I haven't got time to—"

Chuka turned around. "And you'd better hurry."

"Listen, gunfighter—"

"Just do it," Chuka said.

The crack of Jake's carbine riffled through the air again. Chuka looked up at the north tower.

"That's three, now," he heard a man say in the tone of one who had just won a bet. It sounded like Henry.

There was quiet, cold, hushed activity all over the Fort. Soldiers came from their quarters, hustled along by Hahnsbach; there was very little talking. The metallic click of rifles being checked, pistols being waded and tested, could be heard all around him. Chuka gathered up his carbine, canteen and box of shells and started for the door. On the way out he picked up half a loaf of bread and stuck it under his arm.

"Hey!" The cook yelled after him, but Chuka did not reply. He walked around the length of the gallery to the officers' mess and stared into the window. The scene was quiet. A man was on a cot, apparently asleep. John Sheppard and Eve sat in one corner talking. Señora Klietz sat beside the wounded soldier; Helena Chavez sat before the stove, her hands in her lap, staring. Chuka recognized her attitude as the one she had exposed to him in the kitchen. The Ute woman was asleep on the floor.

He stepped to the door, opened it and looked in. "Morning!" He said cheerfully. Everyone snapped around to look at him. "That coffee and hot water will be along in a minute, ma'am," Chuka said to Señora Klietz. "How's the soldier?"

"His fever broke last night," Señora Klietz said, looking at him.

"Think he'll be able to shoot?" Chuka asked.

"It depends on the man," she said, staring at him. Their eyes met. Chuka nodded, shrugging, "Yes, ma'am. It sure does."

He looked at Sheppard. "Coming, John?" He asked. "It won't be long until sunup now."

"Yes—yes, I'm coming."

"Got a gun?" Chuka asked.

Sheppard pulled out an over-and-under Derringer. "That's fine for getting even in a crooked card game; but we'll have to get you something more in line for right now." Chuka smiled, but his attempted joke did not get a response.

John Sheppard stood up. He held onto Evangeline's hand and looked into her eyes. They did not speak. He pressed her hand. Sheppard turned to pick up his coat and hat just as Valois appeared at the door, Captain Carrol behind him.

"Good morning," he said hoarsely. "How is the man this morning, Señora Klietz?"

"He will recover," she said.

"Fine." Valois spoke to the woman. "Captain Carrol, when there is no actual attack, will be here to assist you in any way he can."

The crack of Jake's carbine whined again. "Four," Chuka said, half to himself.

"Who is *that* shooting?" Valois asked.

"Jake Watkins whittling down the odds."

"Still thinking of the odds, Mr. Chuka?" Valois said.

"I'm giving them careful consideration, Colonel," Chuka said. "Ready, John? We'll find you a gun somewhere."

"What are your odds on your chances today, Mr. Chuka?" Valois asked.

"I'd say they were about fifty-fifty," Chuka said with a slow drawl, "with an edge to me—"

John Sheppard had stepped over to the wounded man and picked up his rifle. He crossed to the door, brushed past Valois and stood beside Chuka.

The room had quietened to listen to the exchange between Chuka and Valois. As Valois started to speak, four men came in, shoving past the door carrying a tub of steaming water. Veronica Klietz took over then, and began directing the men. She turned to Captain Carrol.

"I will need all of the bandages and medicines and surgical supplies that you have."

Chuka and Sheppard slipped through the doorway and started across the parade ground. Chuka looked at the sky, for the first time there was a hint of gray.

"Ever fire at a riding man before, John?" Chuka asked.

"No."

"Simple enough," Chuka said. "You aim for the biggest thing you see and the easiest thing to hit, and that's the body. Don't try anything fancy. Just aim to hit and knock him off his horse."

"What if he's only wounded?" Sheppard asked. "Or if I hit the horse and the rider goes down—and gets up?"

"That'll happen more often than not," Chuka said. "If you hit the horse and not the rider, then chances are he'll fort up behind the dead horse. You got to get him before he gets cover."

"I see," Sheppard said. "And the wounded man?"

"If there ain't nothing else to shoot at for the moment, you finish him off."

John Sheppard made a sound in his throat.

"It ain't very Christian, John; but it's a way to get out of this alive."

"Yes," Sheppard said.

There were near the wall. "Where shall I stand?" Sheppard asked.

"It would be better for you, I think, to shoot down. Keep your head down and squeeze off your shot low. Get down between two of those piked logs and rest your rifle in the notch. Swing your gun around a couple of times and see how far you can swing it over and back again—"

"The degree of the arc," Sheppard said, nodding.

"If the rider is thirty feet away from the wall, lead him about three inches—thirty five feet out, lead him about four or five inches. You'll get the hang of it after a couple of shots. Seeing how you miss—"

"How will I know that?"

"That's why I think you'd do better shooting from above, down into them. You can watch for the kick of your lead hitting the dirt on the other side of the rider," Chuka said.

"Yes—yes—I understand that."

"You want to kill as many as you can; but at the same time, you don't want to get killed. So remember, keep your head down. Don't stand up and try for one after you missed him, thinking he's going to get away. He'll only circle the Fort and come around again and let you have another crack at him."

122

"Do you think there is any chance they might change their mind?" Sheppard asked.

"No chance. They've done enough killing already to have the soldiers come down hard on 'em. No, they're going to come in and try—"

"But, they can't hope to win—finally—can they? My God, Colorado is a state in the Union now."

"No, they can't win it all. They lost their chance to keep this place theirs when they made friends with the pilgrims."

"Then why do they attempt to do this now?"

"They're mad; and their pride is hurt. There ain't nothing an Indian hates more than to be pitied. Then too, Sittin' Bull made jerky outa Custer up north this summer. They're fired up."

"If you don't mind my saying so, Mr. Chuka, you sound almost sympathetic," Sheppard said quietly.

"No, I ain't sympathetic. You taking my accountin' of facts and making it sound like sympathy."

"Still," Sheppard said, his tone indicating he wanted to continue the subject, "there are things that have to be considered. For instance—"

"You'd better get on up to the wall now, John," Chuka said over his shoulder, peering out of a gun port. "They're coming in. Looks like about a hundred of 'em."

Jake's extra-powerful carbine was the first to fire. And for a while, a full sixty seconds, his was the only gun firing in the gray dawn, as everyone else had to wait for the first wave to come within range.

Chuka watched closely. Every time the carbine cracked, a rider went down.

"Six men and six guns like yours, Jake," Chuka said to himself, "and we'd give 'em hell."

Chuka raised his carbine and stuck it through the gun port. He picked out a big-chested brave on a little pinto and waited.

He fired.

He waited. A split second later he saw the brave snap back and do a complete flip, over the back of the little horse.

"Well now," Chuka said, and jacked another shell into the chamber.

In the few seconds following, the Indians spread across the plains coming from the rocky nest on the rim of the plains to the northwest. The firing around Chuka became more and more steady, a consistent cracking and explosion.

The sound of the advancing hooves grew louder; the earth shook. Chuka picked out another brave. He fired. The man went down.

Another. A third Indian went down; the horse as well. Chuka saw the animal try to get up and fall back to the ground, screaming and kicking in pain. He wanted to throw a shot at the dumb beast; but he restrained himself and chose another brave.

The Indians were getting close now. He could begin to make out their face markings and their individual dress. Cheyenne, Ute, Arapaho, Sioux, Comanche—

The Indians began to fire, riding in their superb, effortless way, hands free, aiming their rifles, looking as though they would fall from the bare backs of their horses, at any instant, but never falling, and racing in, dead center, straight for the Fort.

The fire from within Clendennon was devastating. One-quarter of the attacking force had never reached the walls of the Fort.

Chuka became vaguely aware of screams behind him. Shouts. Orders. Commands. Pleas for help—for more shells—water—help. Screams for mercy as men were dying in back of him, around him.

The acrid smell of burnt powder reached his nostrils and burned his insides with each breath. But nothing stopped Chuka from his undivided concentration on the selection of the target—aim—squeeze—feel the jolt of the stock on the shoulder. Jack in another shell—select a target—aim—fire—

The first wave had been on the attack for ten minutes when the sun broke out, new and fresh and pale yellow on the frozen land.

Then came the main assault. Chuka felt the earth vibrating under him before the shout of alarm came from the high tower.

He grabbed his canteen, loaf of bread, shells and ran to the east side of the Fort. He reloaded the carbine and set himself. The sun hit him and he blinked.

He changed his position and picked up the closest riders. The remains of the first wave were still circling the Fort. Chuka concentrated on these, shooting counterclockwise as the Indians circled clockwise.

He shot them in the chest, making every one count, watched them knocked off the back of their animals, literally torn from their seats.

Chuka had never seen so many Indians, had never heard so much sustained, steady gunfire, so many men scream, both Indians and white men.

He fired—fired again and again, aiming carefully, knowing his rifle, squeezing the round off, reloading.

The first wave had been merged with the second, the main assault force. The first attack on the morning of November 18th lasted for one hour.

Even when the Indians broke and retreated beyond range, the firing continued as Jake, Henry, Trent, Hahnsbach and Chuka roamed the walls looking for anything that moved, or thought they saw move, killing the wounded and the possum players.

Clendennon had lost nearly one-third of its defenses.

Eight dead, three wounded. There were four in the hospital now; one man lived for an hour with a bullet in his brain, the hole in his forehead like the third eye of evil. He died talking to his mother—babbling disconnected words.

Lieutenant Mack was among the dead, Captain Carrol had been wounded, his left arm useless at his side. The Captain was in such pain that Valois had him quieted with morphine, whereupon the Captain immediately went into shock and lay still on the floor.

"How many did we get?" Valois asked, when he climbed to the high north tower where Chuka, Trent, Jake, Henry and Hahnsbach were still watching for signs of movement among the men strewn around the Fort.

"I counted sixty-seven," Jake said.

"We lost eleven," Valois said. He turned and looked at Chuka. "The odds are six to one, Mr. Chuka. What do you think of that?"

"They're tight," Chuka said, "but I've seen tighter."

"What will happen now?" Valois asked Trent.

"They'll send in a white flag and ask you to give up about noon." The old scout sighed. "Yeah—about noon."

"What are our chances for survival if we accept their offer?"

Trent spit. "None. They'll kill you—everybody—soon as they set eyes on you."

"No," Jake said, checking his supply of shells. "They'll drag out the women and strip 'em buck, then make you watch 'em rape, *then* kill you."

"Yeah," Trent nodded. "Well, that too, of course," he said, as if it had slipped his mind. He looked at Valois. "So, you're the one making the decision."

Valois stepped to the edge of the tower and looked out over the beautiful, dewy, dazzling grass to the mass of Indians beyond range. Their costumes and their movements were as colorful as anything he had ever seen. "When they send in their white flag," Valois said, "tell them I won't talk to anyone but Hanu."

"Hanu won't come out," Trent shook his head.

"You see to it that he does. Tell them I am the commander here, and I will only negotiate with the chief—chief to chief."

"I'll try; but Hanu won't do anything different than what any others would do. They'll just take the message back to him."

"You do as I tell you," Valois said.

"Well, what if Hanu does come out—what'cha got in mind?" Trent asked.

Valois turned to Jake and Chuka. "I'll go out with Trent and talk. When they get within range, kill them."

Trent wiggled his head. "Killing the chief under a truce talk will only rip it wide open, Colonel," Trent said. "Sure that's what you want to do?"

Valois turned, his face as hard as flint. "When the first shot was fired on this establishment, Mr. Trent, it was ripped.

Valois then looked at Chuka and Jake. "Trent and I will be unarmed. Don't miss."

He turned to the steps and hurried down to the ground.

"Well now," Trent said with a twinkle in his eyes, "he's showing up just fine. Just fine."

Chuka and Jake did not hear him. They had seen something else. The old scout followed their gaze. Four soldiers were carrying two litters. There was no mistake who the men upon the stretchers were— Earl Baldwin and Dan Howard, both dead.

"Damn," Trent said.

"Yeah," Jake said in his dour, bitter way. "Damn!"

Chuka said nothing. His eyes were soft, studying the middle distance, as if looking for something on the far side of the fort.

126

Chapter Ten

IT did not take long for the deception Valois planned to spread through the Fort. There were a few who argued against it and wanted to take their chances with a genuine surrender; but the majority agreed with Valois. Their belief was based on faulty knowledge and misunderstanding, thinking that with Hanu dead, the others would refuse to fight. Valois heard this and warned Trent and the others not to explain the difference.

The hours between the first attack and the truce meeting that was to be arranged with Hanu were spent in preparations. Hahnsbach saw to them. The burly Sergeant seemed to be everywhere, seeing that each man's rifle was in good working order, not bore scraped from overheating and thus less accurate, that each man had a full supply of shells, catering to the needs of Señora Klietz and the women taking care of the wounded, checking on the food, seeing that each man was given hot coffee and bread and beef, that all canteens were filled. Everywhere and doing everything, that was Hahnsbach.

At ten in the morning, with the sun climbing and the cold November morning warming up, the Fort ready for another attack, the activity lessened and the men could relax. But their relaxation was not that of complete nonchalance. Their tension remained and showed itself in many ways. The men could not sit; they had to move, do something. Hahnsbach, a veteran for nearly thirty years, had known this and had tried to keep the men busy. Yet there was nothing else to do, but wait. The men's inner tension, however, had to be released and they began to kid among themselves, joking and grabbing each other. Several picked sides and began to pitch horseshoes, a big private and a still bigger private stripped to the waist and began to wrestle. The sun warmed them. They were alive; it was tough luck for the dead ones; but among these that remained, each was sure that he would last it out, that he would see it through. He might be the very last man to live in Clendennon; but somehow—some way— he would live to tell about it.

The unspoken comradeship that had formed in the early hours of the morning when Chuka, Jake, Trent and Henry had arrived at the kitchen together, continued. The four men remained in the high north tower and watched the line of Indians on the distant plains. There wasn't as much movement in their ranks now as there had been soon after the first assault. The men talked and watched the soldiers in the parade ground below. Their talk, their understanding of the situation, grunting answers, making sudden, unrelated remarks, did for the four westerners what the throwing of horseshoes and wrestling was doing for the soldiers. The tension was unbearable; but they were used to it. Their life, their way of thinking, allowed them to go no further, in an effort to do something, than talk about cattle, snow, past brushes with Indians, guns, fist fights they had seen or been in, women they had had, the drunks they had wallowed in and for how long. Talk was good for them because, as a general rule, they were not men who had the time to spare for it.

They all were curious about Chuka's ability with a gun, his fights and his reputation. Chuka told them about the fight with Mark Holly, how he had gotten past Dory and Akins. He did not go into detail; he did not add or subtract. He told them the bare, straight facts because they would add to his account themselves.

At high noon, Chuka saw four riders break from the Indian camp and head for the Fort. They carried no flag, though one rider carried a Comanche lance, the feathers on the tip rippling in the rush of air as the Indians jogged toward the Fort. They stopped at a point half the distance between their camp and the Fort.

The activities in the Fort stopped at once. Every man had climbed onto the walls to watch the approaching braves. One of the many things that Hahnsbach had done was to prepare the horses for Trent and Valois.

Trent turned away from the tower wall and limped down the stairs. Valois was already mounted and waiting for him.

"Open the small gate," Trent said, mounting.

"No, open the main gate," Valois said. "I want them to see our confidence."

"Well, won't hurt none," Trent said.

The big main gate was opened. Valois rode out ahead, Trent right behind him. Valois rode with his back straight, wearing his saber.

The two men did not talk for long, not more than a minute. Then the men at Clendennon could see Trent using sign language; waving his arms at the Indians and they answered him in the same way. Suddenly Trent and Valois wheeled their horses around and headed back for the Fort.

"Did it work?" Chuka asked, calling down from the tower.

"It worked," Valois said. "They're going to bring up Hanu and the three sub chiefs. We have to go back unarmed."

"That's four men," Chuka said.

"What's the matter, gunfighter? The odds too high for you?" Valois asked, stripping off his saber and removing his gun. Trent wanted to keep his knife.

"Everything, Mr. Trent," Valois said.

"Well—just about. I'm taking the sticker. I'll tuck it inside here."

The old scout lifted his arm and inserted the knife blade inside the back of his collar. "There."

Chuka watched from below. "Think you could get one of them with that thing?"

"Why shore," Trent said.

"Don't get Hanu," Chuka said. "Big chiefs like him don't carry weapons. Take out one of the others."

"I'll take the one in the middle. There'll be one alongside Hanu—right?"

"Right," Chuka replied. "I'll get one of the outside ones, and Jake will get the other."

Valois looked up. "Do you still have that Derringer Mr. Sheppard?"

John Sheppard nodded and tossed down the gun. Valois examined it and looked back at Chuka. "I'll take care of Hanu," he said, slipping the gun inside his glove. "Are you ready, Mr. Trent?"

"I guess," Trent said. "You strike first," Trent yelled.

They rode out again. The Indian group did not come out to meet them for nearly fifteen minutes; and then there were five braves.

"Henry," Chuka said, "We're going to need you."

"I ain't much good; but if Jake, here, lemme have a few of them big blow shells of yours—"

Hahnsbach suddenly was beside them. "I am very good," he said, simply.

Henry passed the carbine to Hahnsbach without a word. The five Indians gingerly approached the halfway point. They did not hang back; but they rode cautiously.

The Indians walked the last few hundred feet and stopped before Valois and Trent. Trent started the Indian sign talk, waving his arms in an exaggerated manner, making sure that his right hand was high over his head. Valois sat stiffly, his hands resting easily on the saddle, his fingers only inches away from the Derringer. All the braves, except the old chief, were armed. They carried carbines, and though they were alert, only one of them actually had the gun up.

Trent was in the process of telling the chief they wanted safe passage north, waving his arms in a gentle rolling motion when, as one, the carbines cracked from the tower. Three of the braves fell instantly dead, their eyes rolling back in their heads with a startled, amazed look.

Valois drew the Derringer and fired as Hanu whirled his pony around. He fired twice, catching the old chief in the back of the head.

Trent drew and threw in one motion and caught the last Indian as he squeezed off a shot at Valois, the shot going wild.

The two men whirled around and pounded back toward the Fort. They had not gone a hundred feet when the screaming Indians on the plains behind them started chase.

A group of fifty slipped from their horses where the slaughter of the five had taken place and bent to look after them. The others came on in.

But the Fort was ready for them. The gates slammed shut behind Trent and Valois and were barred by the time the first group of assaulting braves reached the range of the men on the walls.

And it began again.

But this second attack was different from the first, just as Trent and Chuka and the others thought it would be. The Indians flung themselves against the walls of the Fort without thought for their safety. Caution was thrown to the winds. Their outrage at the treachery had taken hold of them. They were no longer fighting a planned attack with waves of men riding in, darting in and out of range, drawing the troopers' fire back and forth, making them miss with their speed and incredible horsemanship, knowing the defending force was but a handful and almost sacrificing men at six, eight, ten to one to gain control of the Fort and the supplies This time they were enraged. They rode straight ahead and fired point blank up the side of the walls. Some flung leather lariats to the top of the poles, and vainly attempted to climb to the top, hand over hand, only to be slaughtered before they got halfway off their horse.

The men within Clendennon looked down on a sea of milling, screaming, shouting, vengeance-ridden Indians. The soldiers hardly could miss once they pointed their guns downward and fired.

Screaming horses and men, the stench of burnt powder, the sight and sound and smell of battle reached Chuka once more as he stood in his earlier position, ground level, shooting through the gun port.

The action was short-lived. The Indians could not take the deadly, cutting fire from the men within Clendennon. They were forced to withdraw, and though there were a few who refused to return to the line beyond range of the Clendennon guns, and died for their lack of caution, most of them retreated.

Once more, after the retreat of the main force, the carbines in the north tower began to crack as the wounded, horses as well as men, were finished off, with special attention shown to possum players.

"How many did we get?" Chuka asked, climbing to the north tower where Jake was once more cleaning out his carbine. "I counted an even fifty."

"Not bad. With those we got already, makes a hundred and seventeen." He looked across the Fort and down on the ground. "Damn near that many horses, too. I never seen such a mess," Chuka said, his voice on edge. Dammit, look at the death—"

Jake glanced up. "Hey, gunfighter."

Chuka snapped around, his face tight.

Jake was grinning at him, easily. The two men looked at each other a minute, then Chuka nodded. "Yeah," he said, "yeah." He relaxed his shoulders. "Yeah."

"How many did we lose?"

"Five," Chuka said. "Ten to one."

"Anybody we know?" Jake asked, bending over his rifle.

"John Sheppard," Chuka said wearily. "I told him to keep his head down—"

Jake said nothing.

Chuka looked out to the line of Indians on the far horizon. "They won't be coming in again—not today."

Jake looked up, across the plains. It was the same line they had established that morning. "No, not anymore today. But we're sure going to catch hell with the sneaky ones crawling in tonight."

"They'll come in like locusts," Chuka agreed.

"I'm going to try something I heard a feller did off the belly of the Rio Grande where he'd homesteaded this place."

"What's that?" Chuka turned and looked down from the tower where Hahnsbach and a detail of men were putting still another corpse, wrapped in a blanket, alongside the others. The line was neat, militaristic, precise. Hahnsbach after nearly half a lifetime of military habit was not going to change, even in the face of death.

Jake was explaining his idea. "Fight fire with fire. Take a torch and wait until you hear an Injun coming. They ain't hard to hear, just locate. When you hear one, throw the torch over the walls and it lights up about one hundred feet all around. This feller from Texas said they stand up and try to hide like naked women, holding their hands—" Jake giggled and bent over his carbine.

"We'd have to kill three times as many as we've killed already to make 'em quit."

"We ain't lacking for shells," Jake said.

"I'm going down to eat," Chuka said. "You coming?"

"No. I ain't hungry," Jake replied, his tone already changing, now that he was going to be alone and would have only his thoughts to chew on—thoughts. Chuka was not yet down the stairs and onto the hard ground before Jake had taken the carbine and began stripping it again, bending over his tasks, whistling softly to himself.

There was no activity around the interior of the Fort now. Chuka walked over to the kitchen and strode in, stopped and stared. Evangeline and Helena were standing before the stove.

"Where are the cooks?" Chuka asked.

Eve looked up at him. Her face was strained, her eyes red from tears. "They were killed in the first attack this morning."

"Eve," Chuka said.

She spun on him. "Don't tell me you're sorry about John," she said bitterly. "I know you're sorry. The whole damn world is sorry."

Helena, quick to respond, stepped forward and put her arms around Eve's shoulders.

Chuka hesitated. "I told him to keep his head down."

"I know—I know," Eve said, her tone softer. "He told me—how you tried to help him. He was very proud of himself."

Eva started to pick up the heavy pot filled with beef soup. "Here, let me take that," Chuka said.

132

"No, I'll do it. You sit down and have coffee or something." Eve's eyes wandered. She turned away her head to avoid Chuka as the tears welled up in her eyes then left the kitchen swiftly.

Helena stood beside the stove. "Now it is my turn," she said, trying to smile at him. She offered Chuka a cup of coffee. "Sit down."

Chuka took the coffee. "Thank you," he said absently, looking out the door, after Evangeline, who carried the heavy pot of beef soup with difficulty.

Helena saw him looking and smothered a deep sigh. She sighed again. "It seems so hopeless. What if—the men in the hospital—what if—they should live?"

Chuka turned and looked at her. "Miss Helena, if you don't mind my saying so, you have been talking that way—well, at least the little you've said to me—" He stopped.

"What way is that?" She asked.

"Dying—and giving up hope."

"Have you not given up hope, Mr. Chuka?"

"No, I haven't," Chuka said, sipping the coffee. "I guess it's just in the way I look at things. Everything alive has the right to go on living."

Helena looked at him. "You are a strange one to be talking about living." She glanced at his gun.

"You mean this?" Chuka pulled out the weapon and looked at it. "Everything alive has got to find its own way of living. This is one way. For me. For a lot of men. It isn't just for killing men, Miss Helena. Rattlers, for instance—me or him."

"Then it does not bother you to shoot the Indians?" Helena asked, her lips on the verge of trembling, and her eyes near tears.

"It bothers me," Chuka said.

"But it is the law—of the—jungle. Kill or be killed."

"Something like that," Chuka said.

"But not quite."

"If I wasn't expected to protect myself, ma'am, why are the Indians out there determined to kill me?"

"Interesting, Mr. Chuka," a voice said from the door.

Chuka spun around. Veronica Klietz stood perfectly straight, her head high, her eyes flashing. She glanced at Helena, once, briefly, saw the tears flooding the girl's eyes, saw, too, Helena's control of them, then turned back to Chuka. She held her hands folded across her stomach. Veronica Klietz was perfectly groomed, not a hair was out of place, her dress spotless. "Hurry with the gruel, Helena. The young private appears to have an appetite in spite of a splintered knee."

"Si," Helena said, turned her back to Chuka and busied herself about the stove. Veronica Klietz had not yet moved, neither had she stopped staring at Chuka. Chuka leaned against a post and stared back over the rim of his coffee mug.

"Good morning," Chuka said.

Veronica did not appear to hear the greeting. She stepped into the kitchen and spoke without looking at Chuka. "And I suppose you also believe in an eye for an eye and a tooth for a tooth."

"No," Chuka said simply.

Veronica Klietz turned slowly and looked him in the eye. There was depth in her look now. "Most men—" She looked at the gun on his hip.

"Gunfighters," Chuka said. "Pistoleros." He nodded his head slightly.

"Pistoleros, then," Veronica Klietz said. "Such people do not usually bother with philosophy."

"I agree," Chuka said.

Veronica held herself up. "You seem to have a high opinion of yourself," she raised one eyebrow, "pistolero."

"I always try to take care of myself; if that's what you mean."

"That is not what I mean."

"And how many pistoleros have you known, Miss Veronica?" Chuka asked, a twinkle in his eyes.

"I have known quite a few men who lived because of their ability with arms, Señor Chuka."

"That's mighty unusual," Chuka said, nodding. Veronica's eyes flashed; but when she spoke, her tone was measured and controlled. "I once knew a handsome young officer in the Emperor's Palace Guards—"

"An officer with a sword, it isn't quite the same—"

"Hush, Sir. Don't be rude. Allow me to finish."

134

Chuka shrugged and smiled, "Yes, ma'am."

"This young man was the finest swordsman in the entire army. He had the finest balance of any that I have ever seen—and when I was a young girl, Mr. Chuka, handsome young officers of the guard were a specialty of mine. Over the years, I developed a keen eye for the finesse—" She paused and looked at Chuka. "Finesse means—"

"I've been to New Orleans, Miss Veronica. I know what it means," Chuka said.

"Oh," Veronica nodded. "This young man of whom I speak was the finest, the most exquisite figure. He was positively beautiful in his uniform. His use of the blade was, well, if you will, like the evil wand of some mythical creature. No one could be compared to him at that time."

"But a pistolero, Miss Veronica—" Chuka tried to interrupt.

"I've forgotten his name now," she went on. "But he was a poor boy. He used his head and his clever tongue to work his way into the inner circles of the Emperor's court, where life was a way of moving from one pleasure to another, without thought or care of worry—except about more and more pleasure. I was madly in love with him; not seriously, mind you, but with the passion of a young girl seeking the most beautiful, the most pleasurable, the most desirable. Well now, living that kind of life, you can well imagine, was not to be done on officer's pay. I was not curious—I didn't care. But slowly, over a period of time, I would hear about duels—oh, duels were forbidden, of course; but it was fashionable, Mr. Chuka. They would take place in secrecy, arranged with elaborate care. Every detail of the ritual was done with formality—even to the bloodletting.

"There, Mr. Chuka, is where my story comes around to you. My handsome young officer with his evil blade was hiring himself out to the highest bidder when two persons found they had to resort to violence to settle their differences. My handsome young officer had wounded more than twenty men—he had killed seven. Killing, Mr. Chuka, was not part of the ritual of the duel as they performed it in my day, but who was to say that in the heat of battle, the hand was thrust with too much emphasis, too little care taken of where the blow was struck? Seven died—about twenty were wounded. A pistolero, Mr. Chuka; only instead of a gun, it was with a sword."

"I still don't see how all this concerns me, ma'am, though it was a mighty interesting story. I met a couple like that, once in San Antonio—"

Veronica cut him off. "He hired his blade—as you hire your gun," she said crisply.

"I've hired my gun. I'm not ashamed of it," Chuka said softly, watching her. "I am still what I am—no more—no less."

"He killed because he was able to kill with impunity, because he knew he was better than his foe, and because he was always protected by a code of honor."

"I can't always depend on giving a man a draw," Chuka said.

"But before any fight, you know you are the better man," Veronica insisted.

"I don't start out to be killed, ma'am."

"What do you call it then, Señor Chuka, when murder is committed, and only the slight difference of a draw separates the facts in the eyes of a man?"

Chuka watched Veronica Klietz with interest. He eased out a sigh, listening, putting the pieces together.

"It would have been far simpler and far easier for your conscience, Mr. Chuka, if you did believe in an eye for an eye and a tooth for a tooth. At least then you would have some excuse—some reason—however weak the position would be. And I should think it would be better than just—hiring your gun to kill—knowing you were the better man."

"You seem to know more about how and why a man does things than the man himself, ma'am," Chuka said easily. "I would be interested in hearing more."

Veronica Klietz's eyes flashed as she looked at Chuka. For a moment, Chuka thought she was going to smile; but instead she looked away. "Would you say that vengeance, however weak that position may be, is more reasonable than the one you now hold?"

"I don't remember stating a position, ma'am," Chuka said. "I just said I didn't believe in an eye for an eye."

"Can you state a position, Sir?"

"You called it philosophy before."

"So I did."

"Which is it going to be? Philosophy or position?"

"You draw a fine distinction between the two?"

"Yes."

"Can you explain that to me?"

"I'm not so sure you want to hear what I have to say. Or that what I would say would make any difference—"

"Are you accusing me of having a—an opinion that could not be changed by a reasonable argument?"

"That would be *your* position," Chuka said.

"And your philosophy, Señor Chuka?"

"I live in a land and in a country and in a time," Chuka said.

Veronica nodded.

"To live, a man has got to be settled on the *way* he wants to live."

"Guided by certain principles," Veronica added, nodding.

"The rules, you called them principles, that guide me in the way I want to live are—simple."

"They are?"

"Truth, ma'am, comes first. Second comes honor. And third, but not in anyways less important than the others, courage."

Veronica started to speak; but Chuka held up his hand.

"Now my position."

Veronica Klietz looked at him sharply, her eyes flashing quizzically. "Yes?"

"My position, ma'am, is to walk with truth, hold onto my honor and find courage to help me over the rough spots."

"And have you found it hard to sustain this position?"

"Harder to hold it a *little* while, than anything else."

"Why?"

"Because we don't always want to tell the truth."

"True."

"And we can't always hold onto our honor, or we'd find ourselves fighting all the time."

"And courage?"

"It's the hardest of all to come by, Señora. And many times when we find our courage, it can be too late, or too little. Chuka looked her in the eye. "Courage is the sneakiest one of them all. It takes courage to face the truth and it takes courage to recognize that your honor is not another man's honor."

Veronica Klietz stepped back. "You are a most amazing man, Señor Chuka."

"That's nice of you to think so, Señora."

"Has this philosophy ever gotten you into trouble?"

"Many times. More than I want to think about."

"Ever thought about giving it up?"

"I don't think I could if I tried. I don't think a man sets out to make himself a certain way. He just grows into it."

"But it would be just as easy, if what you say is true, for a man to grow in an entirely different direction with a different philosophy."

"Just as easy, ma'am. And many do. But you got to remember what I said—one man's truth, or honor or courage isn't the test for another man."

"What about your honor when blackmailing Colonel Valois to ride scout for him?"

"Well now, which was it? Courage on my part to go at all? Truthfulness on my part to ask for the money? Or a lack of honor? Or looking at it the other way, real honor inasmuch as I refuse to take a big risk without proper respect for myself."

"You are an argumentative person, Señor Chuka. Are you sure you haven't talked your victims to death?"

Chuka laughed out loud.

"Come, Helena, Evangeline is all alone."

"Just a minute, Miss Veronica," Chuka said.

"Yes?"

"You didn't finish your story about the handsome young officer."

"Didn't I?"

"What happened to him?"

"He was slain—attacked from behind." She paused and looked at Chuka. "Someone took vengeance."

The two women moved past him and out the door, awkwardly carrying a heavy pot of steaming gruel. Chuka made no move to help them.

"Boy," he said half aloud, shaking his head, "you just been turned inside out—by an expert."

Trent limped in, his eyes red and his eyelids heavy. "Anything to eat? I'm hungry as a bear."

The old man scratched himself and moved around the kitchen, grumbling and mumbling to himself, trying to come awake.

"Lou," Chuka said thoughtfully, "you got a philosophy?"

"Got a what?"

"A philosophy of life."

"You hung over too?" Trent grunted and ignored him.

"I mean it," Chuka said. "You got any special ways of looking at things that you always use as a handy guide?"

Trent still did not answer. He had found the shank of a beef bone and was busy peeling off thin slices with his knife.

"Well?" Chuka demanded.

"What the hell kind of talk is that for this time of day?"

"I'd like to know."

"What?"

"What I asked you. You must have a special way of looking at things. You lived a long time out here. That ain't so easy."

Lou Trent chewed slowly, nodded once, then again, and finally looked up at Chuka. "I ain't never thought about it much."

"But there is something," Chuka said.

"Yeah—I guess so."

"What?"

"I'm straight—and I'm right," Trent said. "I'll give a fair shake. Always have. Got me in trouble lots of times, but I done it. That answer your question?"

"Where's your whiskey, Lou?" Chuka said amiably. "I figure I got one more coming to me before I check out."

"Be right with you as soon as I get something to eat."

"To hell with the food," Chuka said. "Let's get to it."

Trent thought a moment, then nodded decisively.

"You're right, gunfighter; I warn't hongry anyway. Let's fling one."

Chapter Eleven

THE scavengers began to appear in the middle of the afternoon. For a while everyone within the Fort tried to ignore their ugly presence. But the clawing, lunging, awkward beating of wings, their obscene screams could not be denied. As if the morbidity of the scene had drawn them to the walls, each man at Clendennon looked and then immediately wished he hadn't.

The men and the women were exhausted. They moved within the walls as if in shock, their movements slow and unhurried, their eyes seeing nothing. The reality of the situation was crowding down on them. The line of dead, two lines really, one within the walls, the other on the outside; the threat of more Indians to come from the far rims of the plains where they waited; the arrival of the scavengers—all this made the battle a reality.

Everyone within the walls of Clendennon wondered if he would be dead within twenty-four hours.

Valois shot one man dead as he tried to open the main gate, screaming and shouting to anyone that would listen, pleading that surrender was the only hope.

This bitter scene shocked some of the others for a while, awakening forgotten anger and hate. There was some talk, quickly crushed by their own inner defeat, about shooting Valois.

The day wore on. It was the longest day any man in Clendennon had ever spent. Once Valois, after shooting the man at the gate, attempted to arouse the men from their deepening sense of doom by shouting at them. Both he and Hahnsbach walked among the survivors and demanded attention. Hahnsbach used his fists on one man, hitting him so hard the man was out cold for an hour afterward. But no one stood up to Hahnsbach; no one cared.

Hahnsbach looked at Valois. There was fear in his eyes, not so much because he feared death in the hands of the Indians, but because his effort to arouse the men had failed. It was as if lifetime habits were deserting him.

Valois hung on, doggedly. He opened new boxes of ammunition, carrying them to the men at their posts, ordered the horses in the stables slain. Hahnsbach shot them all, except the state teams and Chuka's stallion. Both men worked together, preparing the ammunition room, setting the powder and shot and shells in a tight group and setting a fuse as well. They destroyed all papers and dispatches, burned the money in the safe and broke the guns, slamming them on the chopping stump, breaking the stocks.

Quite unexpectedly the sun grew very hot in the late afternoon. It would not last, but sometimes in November, like October, only less frequently, the heat begins to build. In the heat, the stench of the dead began to float into Clendennon many of the men wretched and sagged back to their sitting positions, weaker; the last of their will draining from them.

The screams of the scavengers became more penetrating. One man stood on the walls and began to fire rapidly into the waddling creatures. The flock beat the earth with their wings, rose a few feet in the air, then came back down to rest, not ten seconds later, to continue their morbid feast. The man redoubled his efforts, unaware that he was crying, that tears of fear, hate, anger were streaming down his face. Finally he stopped shooting and sagged to the floor of the walk.

Jake and Henry remained in the north tower. They became as silent as the men below them, knowing what was coming. They expected it and just sat and waited, watching the line of Indians on the rim of the plains. No one had any hope for help to arrive. It would have taken the combined commands of Wallace and Garland to fight the Indians with any success.

The dispatches, the reports Trent had made to Valois, who in turn had forwarded to the commanding officer at Wallace, would not be acted upon. There was no way for Wallace and Garland to know that Clendennon was in trouble.

More than a few of them thought about trying to sneak out when dark fell, deserting the Fort and saving themselves. To stay was certain death; but they also knew that to go was death as well. Only if one was caught outside, death would come more slowly.

The earlier feeling each had had, that regardless of what happened at Clendennon, he would survive, was gone. They could no longer put off the facts and the reality of their condition.

There was no one, by the time the sun began to drop, that believed he would see another sundown. They could not run; they could not hide, and to fight would be vain and useless.

Chuka, as much as he drank Trent's liquor, could not get drunk. He could not even get to the point where he felt reckless and arrogant. He never reached the point which, in the past, always had been able to get him loose and grinning.

Trent was so drunk, he was talking to himself by the time the sun nearly was touching the edge of the plains, backlighting the Indians, showing them as black figures, shadows, without color or definition. The whiskey was gone. Chuka looked down at the two empties on the ground before him, raised one boot-heel and came down with a kick, shattering both bottles. The pieces of glass reflected the last weak rays of the sun.

He stood up, checked his gun and walked back into the stables, into the stall with the stallion. He pulled the horse's ears, talked softly to it and patted the big animal on the neck. The horse nuzzled him.

Chuka pulled out his pistol and took a step back. There was no emotion as he rocked the hammer back.

Crack! Crack!

Jake's carbine, its heavy overloaded shells exploded in the air.

"They're coming in again—they're coming in again—"

The voice penetrated through the hard clot of resignation in Chuka. He stared at the stallion, then at the gun in his hand.

"No!" He said, his teeth clenched, his gut hard, the bitterness of his will to survive rising like a flood within him. "Nooo!" He screamed.

He turned and fled through the stables, sweeping past Trent, who was trying to get up from the ground. Chuka skidded to a stop, spun around, grabbed the old man by the shoulder and lifted him upright with one hand. He slapped him across the face and shouted into Trent's ear.

"Get up there! Move—get up there and defend yourself; or I'll blow your guts out right now!"

He slapped the old man again. The eyes spun dizzily, wavered. Chuka slapped him again.

Trent straightened.

Chuka turned and ran for the wall, snatching up a rifle that had been cast aside and slammed into a notch.

Then he settled into his old self. The years of gun handling, the years of facing death, the years of building up an iron will to survive, all this took over the big man and he began to fire with the same methodical coolness as he had always done.

The resistance within Fort Clendennon began slowly. At first there were only five gunners shooting—Jake, Henry, Valois, Hahnsbach and Chuka. Then another joined the five. Trent stood on the ground, a six-gun in each hand, standing well back from the wall and sighting carefully—one hand, then the other—left hand—right hand—left hand—right hand—

The fire power in Clendennon picked up. Here and there the men began to stand up and aim, sight—fire—working on reflex at first, many of them unaware that they were firing. As Chuka's iron will had snapped him out of his lethargy, their military training was working, discipline stepping in, controlling their actions.

The attack was timed perfectly. The onrushing Indians had the sinking sun at their backs and knowing this, they took full advantage of it. They came in straight and true.

Clendennon's fire power was at its maximum effort by the time the Indian's reached the walls. The men met the assault with deadly accuracy. The first wave of Indians was completely wiped out. The horses turned and bolted from the walls and charged around wildly, milling with the second and third waves, creating confusion. This, as much as the firing from Clendennon, snapped the back of the drive. There were a few, however, that did survive and gain the base of the walls and using lariats again, attempted to pull themselves to the top. There these few were met with point-blank fire. The muzzles of rifles and six-guns jammed into their faces and fired.

The attack broke in confusion rather than rout; and the Indians retreated, riding beyond range. But they did not retire to the distant line of their camp, nor did they dismount.

Chuka turned away from the wall and reloaded. Only then did he look up and sweep over the Fort with a glance.

Henry was down, crumpled in a heap at the base of the tower where he had fallen. Trent was dead, half of his head blown off. Hahnsbach was trying to get to the hospital door, blood streaming from a neck wound. He dropped to the ground the moment Helena and Evangeline Sheppard reached him.

Then Chuka saw Valois across the parade grounds. The young officer was standing, reloading, his fingers moving without looking as he stared after the line of Indians. He turned, saw Chuka and waved, then started a slow walk around the top of the wall. At one north tower, Jake came down the stairs and joined Valois. Together they walked over to Chuka.

"How many left?" Chuka asked.

"This is it," Valois said.

"What are you going to do with the women?" Chuka asked.

"It's up to them," Valois said.

"We'd better ask them—quick," Chuka said. "We ain't got much time before they hit again."

"And the wounded?" Valois asked.

"That's strictly a military decision," Chuka said "But you know as well as I do what will happen to them—anybody that's alive and kicking."

Valois nodded grimly. "Let's talk to the women. They did not look at the dead around them but kept their eyes forward and walked straight to the door of the hospital.

Veronica Klietz met them at the door. One look at their faces and she knew. "We have already decided," they said.

"Well?" Chuka asked, when Valois did not speak.

"We will join you on the walls."

"And if they take you alive, Miss Veronica, do you know what to expect?"

"They will not take us alive."

"What about them?" Jake said, pointing to the wounded.

Chuka looked at the faces around him. "I ain't going to do nothing about it," he said through his teeth.

"The merciful thing would be—" Veronica Klietz could not finish her thought.

Valois turned aside from the group. "It has to be done," he said. "All of you had better get to the walls—I'll stay here."

Chuka directed the women through the doorway. When the Ute woman started to move after the others, Chuka stopped her. "You too?" He asked, speaking her language.

"Me more than the others, dog-wolf," she said.

"Find yourself a gun," Chuka said, pressing his lips together.

Jake walked after, the women, leaving Chuka and Valois alone. Chuka watched the young Colonel stand facing the wall.

"Can you do it?" Chuka asked.

144

Valois was a long time answering, "Yes—I can do it."

"They're all unconscious," Chuka said easily. "They won't know what hit them."

Chuka hesitated a moment, then without another word, walked through the door. He was halfway across the parade ground when he heard the first shot. He stopped still in his tracks.

Another shot. The others were perfectly still, not moving, not turning to look.

A third shot—then a fourth—a fifth. And then it was over.

Chuka walked over to the four women and Jake. "Keep your head down," he said choking back his anger, "and aim carefully. I'll tell you now, it would be better to keep one back—for—" He could not finish. "But that's your decision to make."

He stepped past them and climbed to the walls. He gathered up four six-guns from the dead, checked and reloaded them, putting them on the floor beside him, within easy reach.

Jake returned to the tower; Valois walked to the comer of the west wall just above the gate and stood alone.

When Chuka looked up from loading the last gun he saw Helena Chavez down on her knees, a string of beads in her hands, Veronica Klietz standing over her. When Helena was finished, she stood and Veronica Klietz knelt down and confessed to the younger woman.

The Ute woman and Evangeline stood together, watching the not too distant line of Indians. The scavengers returned and began to scream. The sun was nearly gone, and what remained of it was dropping fast.

Valois turned from the wall and, moving quickly, set fire to the buildings and the piles of stores as he and Hahnsbach had planned. In a matter of seconds, the flames began to spread, and thick black smoke began to curl upward in the darkening sky.

Valois yelled at Jake and Chuka from the ground. "The last one." He turned and pointed to the storehouse where the ammunition supplies were waiting and ready for demolition. "Shoot that big keg out front."

Jake and Chuka waved that they understood, and Valois returned to his position over the main gate.

Veronica Klietz moved closer to Chuka, a big black pistol looking awkward and clumsy in her delicate white hands.

"Who were your people, gunfighter?" She asked.

"Just folks."

"Where did they come from?"

"Pa came from Georgia; Ma came from Mississippi."

Veronica Klietz said nothing for a moment. "My mother was a second cousin to the Austrian Emperor. My father was Spanish nobility."

"It don't help either one of us, ma'am, at the moment."

Veronica Klietz looked sideways at Helena Chavez. "Her father is Augustino Chavez, one of the richest men in Mexico—and her mother was born in Madrid, the daughter of an escort of the Duke of Alba."

"You giving me the blood lines like a horse trader, ma'am," Chuka said slowly. "Why?"

"Because," Veronica Klietz said, "I'm putting her life into your hands."

"That ain't going to be very long."

"For whatever you wish, Sir."

"I don't follow you."

"You asked me once, Mr. Chuka, why we were turning back to the south and not going on to the east. Helena was given by her father to a man in New York—"

"With or without her permission?"

"She had nothing to say about it."

"High-handed, ain't it?"

"Helena thought so. She rebuked the proposal. She refused to carry on with it. I had no alternative but to return her to her father's house—"

"What would happen then?"

"A convent," Veronica Klietz said.

"Would that be done without her permission as well?"

"She would have no other recourse. No other arrangement could be made, once it became known that Helena had rebuked her father's given word."

"Did she know all this—about the convent—when she turned the other feller down?" Chuka asked, watching the Indians.

"Yes. She knew what she was doing."

"That says a lot for her, wouldn't you say, ma'am?"

"I am an old woman, Mr. Chuka. I have lived my life, regardless of what you may think of it, according to the traditions and customs of my people. It is hard for me to explain why I have done some of the things in my past, admitting to a certain inadequacy—a less than perfect point of view—But I did them honestly with no intent to harm. It is just as hard, Mr. Chuka as it is for you to explain to me your reasons for being a pistolero."

Chuka nodded. "I can see that. Heard a feller say once, a sailor from a ship when I was in New Orleans, been all over the world, that there was a place halfway to China where they didn't even believe in the Lord Jesus, but worshipped a stone idol instead. But he said they were brave people. And soft and gentle."

Chuka sighed, "I don't understand it completely, Miss Veronica. I guess the way a man is raised don't make much difference if they can come up to the situation—"

"Death."

"Yessum, death. And face it down."

They were both silent a moment, watching the Indians as they began to circle and parade their ponies back and forth in the last of the daylight, working themselves up for another lunge on the Fort.

Veronica Klietz suddenly turned on Chuka and put her hand on his arm. Her voice was desperate. "Can you escape this, Chuka? Is there a way out?"

"No, ma'am," Chuka said, avoiding her eyes.

"For yourself—are you going to try?"

"Miss Veronica," Chuka said, "ma'am, there's three men and four women."

"Then you will stand and die?"

"I'm going to do my level best, Miss Veronica to stay alive just as long as I can."

Veronica Klietz took a deep breath and shuddered, "As I will do. But should you see the outcome, Mr. Chuka, I want you to be merciful—and do it—when neither of us is looking."

Chuka did not answer. Veronica turned and walked to Helena Chavez. The two women embraced.

Chuka looked around at Eve. "How you doing, Eve?" He asked with a smile.

Eve looked up at him. Her face was still red from her sobbing over John Sheppard. "I can face it," she said. "I don't want to. I want something else." She caught herself. "We were going to live in a big house on the banks of the Ohio. Johnny came from Ohio."

"I'm sorry, Eve," Chuka said.

"I'm sorry too, Chuka. But it's just as well this way. Lord! I don't know how I could pick up, and go on and hope some more if we came out of this."

Then suddenly, she heaved a big sigh, turned away a moment, then looked back at Chuka. "Well, if this is going to be it, I'm going out kicking and screaming. The first son of a bitch that puts a finger on me—" She shrugged and turned her eyes back to the Indians.

The Indians stopped circling and began their charge. "Aim low— hit anything that moves," Chuka said to the women.

He spared one last look around the Fort. The flames of the burning stores billowed higher and higher. It was nearly dark, getting cold again. The heat from the fire was just right on Chuka's back. He saw Jake and waved. The tall man waved back. Then Valois lifted his hand to Chuka before turning to the gunshot flag that had flown all night. He came to attention, snapped a salute, then turned back to the walls.

The Indians did not come in with a rush this time. They rode at a pace hardly more than a jog, sure now, taking their time, aiming carefully with their return fire. Those in the front ranks were cut down by the wicked and deadly fire of Valois, Jake and Chuka. They hit everything they aimed at. The big *crack!* of Jake's carbine sounded again and again and again—

Valois was standing sideways, his back straight, careful of his position, arm extended, as if on a rifle range, firing with the same deadly accuracy as Jake.

Chuka shot with his wrist, shooting with the sureness of ten thousand practice rounds, his vision covering a wide are, seeing the approaching Indians from the corner of his eye, throwing his wrist in a rolling motion and squeezing the trigger. There were no mistakes; he was sure, confident, snapping left and right, shooting with the speed and accuracy of the true gunfighter. They were all exposed now.

148

Jake, Valois and Chuka, standing high on the skyline of the walls, three guns defiantly ripping out against the pressing mass of Indians and horses below.

The women were firing; but it was useless. No one had hit anything except the ground. The Ute woman had given up completely and stood in the open on the pike tips, inviting the Indian's fire. She was hit a half-dozen times before she had stood straight up, then fell down beside Eve, who hesitated a moment before returning to her awkward handling of the gun. Eve used both hands on the heavy six-gun, as did Veronica Klietz and Helena Chavez.

Now there was silence from the north tower, almost as loud as the big carbine Jake had so lovingly taken care of; silence that spelled the tall man's doom. Jake was nowhere in sight when Chuka glanced up.

Evangeline Sheppard screamed and reeled back from the piked logs, struggling to gain her footing, fell from the catwalk and landed hard on her neck. Even in the screaming noise of the battle, Chuka could hear her neck snap.

The Indians were scaling the walls. Several had already gotten inside and were attempting to open the big gate.

Valois stepped back to the edge of the catwalk over the gate and fired straight down. He hit three of the Indians on the top their heads, then calmly stepped back up to his notch and continued to fire.

The heat of the flames behind Chuka was so intense he could hardly stand still. The Indians were swarming freely up the walls now.

In the half-light, the flickering red glow of the flames, Chuka saw four braves with blades approaching Valois. They rushed him—Valois fired twice. Two fell. Chuka fired from halfway across the parade ground and a third went down.

The fourth Indian dropped lightly to the ground, leaving Valois standing alone, propped against the piked poles. Then Chuka saw the blood on Valois' neck and the final shot squeezed off as he fell to the ground.

Chuka turned around. They were coming over his wall.

He grabbed two of the guns he had prepared and fired, snapping both his wrists. He cleaned the wall.

Chuka turned to Veronica and Helena. Veronica was face down on the catwalk, blood all over the back of her head. Everything inside Chuka rebelled at that moment. His teeth clenched; his lips curled back. He was half-crouched, waiting, watching the Indians pour into the parade grounds below him.

And then instead of firing, he stepped back into the shadows and hugged the walls. He dropped down out of sight and crawled to Helena's side. "Stay down and shut up!" He said, his sweating, dirt-streaked face reflecting the flames.

She looked at him, then down at Veronica Klietz and started to scream. Chuka reached out and with one hand, covered her mouth, pulling her down beside him in the same motion. They were deep in the shadows of the catwalk, back up against the wall. It was dark now, with only the flames of the rapidly spreading fire to light the scene.

Chuka did not move for several minutes. It seemed to him that he did not breathe the whole time. Helena, pulled tightly down against him in the shadows, ceased to resist and began to cry, her tears falling onto Chuka's fingers. He eased his grip, and when he saw she was not going to cry out, took his hand away.

Finally, he saw what he had been waiting for. Two braves were circling the Fort, working their way toward Chuka's position, firing one shot into the head of every body they found.

Chuka studied the milling, shouting Indians below him. No one was paying attention to the two braves administering the coup de grace. Their whole intent was to fight the fire and prevent it from getting to the ammunition stores.

The steady, uneven firing of the two braves continued as they moved from body to body. Chuka raised his gun.

"Lie perfectly still," he whispered into Helena's ear. "If you move, you'll be dead two seconds later."

She did not respond.

"Do you understand—it is my life too!" He hissed.

She nodded, her head still down.

The two braves were on the west wall now. Stop and shoot—stop and shoot—stop and shoot—

Chuka set himself. The Indians drew closer. Chuka raised the gun and took careful aim. Suddenly he relaxed and lowered the gun. Never before in his life had he taken careful aim with a six-gun.

He took a deep breath and waited.

150

One step—two steps—three-

Chuka snapped up the gun and fired. One brave fell. Then Chuka forced himself to wait. The second Indian jerked around and tried to cover himself by backing against the wall. Only then did he raise his rifle to fire.

Chuka fired again—snapping his wrist as before.

The Indian slumped to catwalk. The shots had been evenly paced; there was no difference in the timing.

Chuka leaned down beside Helena. "There is only one way now for us to escape. Do you understand me?"

"Si—yes."

"I must work my way on around the catwalk, and continue to fire. Do you understand?"

"Yes."

"I want you to go to the first brave—and strip his clothes—his blouse, headdress, his breech clout and leggings."

Helena shrank back.

"You must do it!" Chuka hissed. He indicated Veronica. "She told me you had refused to go to New York and marry a man. Were you just having the tantrum of a spoiled brat—or are you a woman who knows her mind?"

Helena's face tightened.

"I won't leave you here," Chuka said. "And you can't hope to escape unless you do as I tell you. Do you want to kill me as well?"

"What shall I do," Helena asked, her voice becoming firm, "once I have his clothes?"

"Strip down raw and put them on," Chuka said coldly.

"Then strip the other one for me."

He did not wait any longer. He turned and fired once in the air and then crawled into the darkness, keeping well back in the shadows, watching the scene below him.

The fire was getting out of control; the flames were spreading to the outer walls and the stables. Chuka almost bolted when he heard the frightened cry of the stage team and his own stallion; but he held himself in check and continued crawling around the upper edge of the walls, firing, spacing his shots as evenly as he could.

151

He was reloading when he saw a shadow move before him.

Chuka lunged from his sitting position and fought for the brave's throat, caught it between his two thumbs and pressed down, hard. Suddenly there was a searing pain in his side, and he knew he had been cut. How badly he did not know or care. The brave had not uttered a sound.

The pain grew to unbearable intensity almost at once, but the gunfighter forced himself to reload and continue his crawl around the catwalk.

He did not circle the Fort completely. The fury of the Indians below him, in their attempt to save the ammunition, gave him confidence that they were not aware of anything except the fire and the threat of the fire reaching the ammunition.

Chuka took the time to feel his wound. His fingers entered the fleshy, bloody gash that had cut deeply, but not critically, into the large back muscle just under his left arm. He tried to raise his arm, found that he could with great difficulty and pain, and did not try again. If the time came when he was forced to use the arm he would put it to the test.

He worked his way back around the edge of the catwalk, still in the shadows, crawling over the bodies of several soldiers he had missed coming down, and stopped suddenly as something ghostly white moved before him.

He jerked up the gun, ready to fire and spring over the wall, when his vision was sharpened by a sudden leap of flames.

Helena Chavez was kneeling down, her back against the wall struggling to remove her petticoat without rising above the protective shadows of the catwalk.

Chuka crawled forward and attracted her attention.

She stopped. Chuka moved to her side and gripping the cloth in his hands, ripped the seams. Helena then tore the clothing from her body. Only once did she look at Chuka as she pulled on the Indian buckskin. Nude, she watched his eyes and returned his stare without a word.

She pulled the breech cloth over her hips and pulled tight on the waist string of the leggings, then put on the blouse, her full breasts swinging slightly as she shimmied into it.

"Now me," Chuka said.

Her eyes blazed for a moment; but she did as she was told, coming forward swiftly and beginning to pull at his boots. He could see her lips pressed tightly together as she put the boots to one side and moved to his shirt. Then she saw the wound in his side. Helena opened her mouth; but Chuka had his hand over it before she could utter a sound.

"I'd do it myself," he said.

She put her hand over his lips and pressed him down gently and quickly, effortlessly stripping him.

She moved into the darkness and returned a moment later with the second brave's clothing and began to dress the big man. There was no hint of false modesty in her face when she helped him with the legging.

The blouse was difficult because of the wound; but Chuka refused to have her do anything to the arm. The open wound, still bleeding, was left untended inside the blouse.

Chuka buckled his gun-belt and picked up the last of the loaded guns he had prepared before the attack. He slipped it into the holster and automatically, without thinking, drew and tested the weight of the weapon against his leg.

Then Chuka reached inside the blouse with his good hand and brought out fingers covered with blood. He motioned her to come to him, and then smeared her face and neck and arms with his own blood. She remained perfectly still. In a few seconds and with a few more smears of his fingers, her milk white skin was transformed into deep brown. Even in the firelight, she looked as dark as an Indian. He motioned her to do the same thing to him.

Only at this moment did she waiver.

"Chuka," she said.

"Do it, dammit!" He said in a hoarse whisper.

She shook her head. He reached inside his blouse again and wet his fingers, smearing his face. Toward the end, she directed him, then finally finished covering his face.

He began to move, then stopped. Helena mover her head and Chuka saw the long hair. It was too long and too full, but if she parted it into two halves—

She did this at once and then slipped on a headband.

Helena looked up at him for approval. He nodded.

Once again, he was ready to move when he noticed her rings. Two large diamonds on one hand, a bright red ruby on the other. He reached over and slipped them from her fingers, shoving them into his holster.

"Why can't we drop over the walls?" She asked, stopping his as he started to move toward the stairs.

"Why would one of them drop over the walls, when all he has to do is walk out the gate?" Chuka asked.

"But—"

"Have you looked over the wall?"

Helena eased her head up to the nearest notch between the log spikes. What had seemed like several hundred Indians inside the Fort walls was actually only a few. At least another hundred and fifty remained just outside, still mounted, watching the fire, waiting for it to be put out.

She slipped back down and started to walk with Chuka, stopped near Veronica's body, dropped quickly to her knees, crossed herself, stood and walked with him to the stairs.

"We're going to get a couple of the ponies," Chuka said, standing in full view for the first time, holding Helena's arm and forcing her to stand still. "See those two pintos over by the gate?"

She nodded and whispered, "Yes."

"Just walk as natural as you can, and do what I do. If anything happens—and you start to—if they look like they're going to get us—I'll—"

"I know. I understand. I have already asked for your forgiveness. "

"Can you ride bareback?"

"Yes."

"Don't be alarmed by anything I do. Just get to that horse, get on it, and wait for the explosion."

"Explosion?"

"All right," Chuka said, without answering her question, "just walk easy."

They stepped off the catwalk and walked down the stairs, turned away from the fire the moment they touched the ground. Helena stumbled over something. Chuka reached out and quickly grabbed her.

Helena uttered a prayer. When Chuka looked down, his face froze as he stepped over the body of Stuart Valois, face down in the frozen ground.

They reached the horses. There was movement all around them; riders rode back and forth through the gate, more of them coming in than going out. "Walk your pony out the gate and hug the wall. Turn right as soon as you get out there — and keep moving. But *don't run!*"

"What are you going to do?"

"Move."

Helena swung easily to the back of the small, well-shaped pinto and walked through the gate, turned to the right, found a deep dark hole where the light from the fire could not reach her and kept moving.

Chuka took the lead of the pony in his hand and looked around. He saw the keg of powder Valois had, pointed out to him. The fire was getting closer to the ammunition stores, and the Indians, realizing there was no hope of putting out the fire and saving the Fort, sought to escape with as many boxes of shells as they could, running into the storehouse and returning with the precious ammunition for their guns. All else could be lost — if the shells for their guns could be salvaged.

Chuka waited until the mound of boxes outside was what he thought would be about half of that inside the storehouse. The keg of powder was buried beneath the squared shell casings.

He looked around, walked the pony to the edge of the gate, drew the gun casually and fired into the keg from the shadows.

He was blown down and nearly lost the lead on the pony as the animal bolted; but he hung on with his good arm. The animal came to a stop at the far end of the Fort.

Chuka looked back. The Indians on the outside were scattering backward into the night.

Helena was at his side then. She slipped from the back of the pony and caught him as he was about to sag to the ground. With the last of his strength, Chuka, with Helena's help, swung onto the Indian pony's back.

Helena's horse reared, but once she had settled the animal, she took the lead of Chuka's pinto and began to move into the darkness.

She did not hurry; she was unafraid. Helena Chavez, for the first time in her life, was completely and totally unafraid of the future. She looked back at Chuka and she knew that.

Near dawn the next morning, in a deep brushy thicket, hidden and protected, they awoke.

"We must get you to a doctor," Helena Chavez said.

"Cut off the blouse," Chuka replied.

Helena slit one side of the blouse and eased the buckskin over his shoulder.

"Now look at it," he said. "What color is it?"

"Red."

"What kind of red?"

"Dark—dark red."

"Not black?"

"No, it is definitely red."

"Any scabby looking stuff around the edges?"

"No."

"Anything crawling in it?"

"Crawling?" Helena's voice quavered.

"Maggots," Chuka said.

"No, it is just dried, dark red."

"No pockets in it of any kind—like a thin skin grew over something inside?"

"No—it is just dark—dark red," Helena said, her voice breaking off.

"Now here's what you're going to do," Chuka said. "Make a little fire, not much, heat the blade of the knife until it gets too hot to touch, then scrape all that dried blood out of there until it's bleeding again."

"You are insane!" Helena said.

"Dammit, do like I tell you. That caked blood is dirty. The Indian that wore this blouse maybe didn't take a bath for a year—and what about my own dirty fingers going in there last night?"

"I will do it," Helena said, clenching her teeth.

It took her an hour to get the blade ready and another hour to clean out the wound. When the clotted blood was scraped away and the wound bleeding, Chuka had the knife heated once more. This time hotter, nearly red—and using the lead of a bullet to bite on, screamed through clenched teeth as Helena applied the fire brand.

Chuka passed out. He did not stay unconscious long; and when he came out of it, he looked up at Helena.

"Feel my forehead."

She did so at once, placing her palm on his face.

"Feel hot?"

"No."

"Did you finish the job while I was passed out?"

"Yes."

"Good girl. I knew I was going to pass out and I meant to tell you beforehand, so you wouldn't get scared and so you'd go ahead and seal it up while I was unconscious. I can't take pain—I just go out—like a candle."

Then Chuka smiled. "We made it," he said. "I didn't think we would; but here we are. And you'll be with your father in no time at all."

"What will you do?"

Chuka hesitated. "Well—I have to see a man in Montana country."

"And then what?"

"Depending on what happens there, I might give it all up."

"A pistolero hanging up his guns?" She asked.

"I'll hang up my guns, Miss Chavez, when I don't think I'll need 'em anymore. I can't see that happening until after I see a man in Montana."

She watched him, watched his eyes. Helena saw them grow hard and distant. "Where were you going when you came to Fort Clendennon?"

"Montana."

"Your friends, Jake and Henry, as well?"

"Yes," Chuka said slowly, "my friends and me were going to Montana to see a man." Then he took a deep breath. "They wouldn't have been at Clendennon if it wasn't for this—man. Neither would I." He stopped.

"Chuka," Helena Chavez said softly, "take me with you."

"No."

"I want to go with you."

"No."

"A convent, Chuka."

"You don't understand," Chuka said. "I'm going to Montana—to—it won't be—"

"I think I understand," she said softly.

"No."

"Take me with you," she said again.

"It won't work worth a damn," he said. "I don't know what's going to happen up there—when I get there."

"Is that the only reason?"

"No," he said slowly. "You're under pressure now. I just saved your life. We went through something terrible together. It makes us close, for the moment—right now. But later—I haven't got a place—or money or position. Just—just my guns. And I don't think that's much to offer." He bit his lower lip and then grinned, a hard, ironic gleam in his eyes. "I even lost the thousand I jacked from Valois."

"Chuka—"

"No, don't argue with me," he said, his voice hardening. I want you to understand that you and I could probably raise hell for a while. But even if I get past that man in Montana, I couldn't ask someone like you to live—to live the way I'm going to have to live, for a coupla years anyway."

"Would you take help from me?"

Chuka didn't answer. "There is something else, too. There would come a time, maybe after we had children, that you would want to see your family. I wouldn't fit into that life, Helena."

"Veronica respected you."

"But I can't depend on others being like her. She found respect for me—and it was under pressure too. You would get tired of my way and want the old way. It wouldn't mix."

"They would respect you if it was honorable between us."

Helena took the .44 from the holster and dug her fingers inside. She held out the two diamond rings and then dug for the ruby. She held them in her palm and looked at them. "In my country, a man expects a woman to bring a dowry."

She put them on Chuka's chest.

He looked at her and then at the rings, picking them up one at a time. "I wouldn't want you to go back to see your family or have them come to see us until we were fixed up—so that when they came and sat down, they would eat decently."

"All right. Not until then," she said. "I promise. And the word is sworn to you."

She smiled at him and started to lean over to kiss him; but Chuka held back. "One more thing," he said.

"Yes?"

"Before anything else, I'm going to Montana—and that will be the last—"

"We will go to Montana, and that will be the last, pistolero."

"I promise," Chuka said, "and the word is sworn to you."

Helena kissed him. When she sat back, she looked deep into his eyes. "May I ask you a question?"

"All right."

"What is your name?"

"Chuka." He frowned. "Sam Halsey, ma'am," he said with a grin.

They moved out of the thicket three days later. There was no threat to them. Easily, talking, they moved steadily north, straight toward the Montana country, through the first of the storms, digging into the high drifting snow, purposefully—a man and a woman seeing into the future, when the man would be done with his past, not yet, but soon. The man known as Chuka, the gunfighter, the pistolero, the sugar gun, would be finished—it ended, really, at Clendennon—

...When the first reinforcements arrived from Forts Wallace and Garland, there were no survivors. Not a living thing could be found. The dead lay within and without the charred walls of the Fort (it was burned to the ground); the evidence of the bitterness of the battle to be found even in the poisoned water of Fort Clendennon's well.

We have positive proof that there were only three women at Fort Clendennon at the time of the attack. Señora Klietz, Señorita Chavez and Evangeline Sheppard; there were three female corpses uncovered at the site. Individual identification was impossible and every step was made to separate the identities. This proved beyond the means of man. The bodies were taken and buried with the rites of two religions, in a common grave, with one head marker and the inscription as follows:

SEÑORITA HELENA CHAVEZ

SEÑORA VERONICA KLIETZ

MRS. JOHN T. SHEPPARD

THEIR SEPARATE SOULS KNOWN ONLY TO THEIR GOD

Those Indians who were not killed in the attack on Fort Clendennon were successfully pursued by the U.S. Army troops and they are now, at this writing, being prepared for their journey to a reservation in the State of Florida.

Your Excellency, it is my unhappy duty to inform you that every shred of evidence has been examined by a board of six officers, two medical, two duty, two staff, to see if a further search for the person of Señorita Chavez is justified. The board was unanimous in its findings. No further search was recommended. It was the finding of the board, further, that the death of Helena Chavez occurred at some unknown instant during the attack on Fort Clendennon which took place on the 17th and 18th of November, 1876.

As a final testament to this fact, I direct your attention, Excellency, to a full and complete record and transcript of the individual questioning of the captured Indians. To the man, they swear that no one escaped. All within the walls of Clendennon died in its defense.

Yours very truly,
Zachiriah Joe Bridge
General, U.S.A.

Biography

Richard Jessup (01/01/1925 – 10/27/1982) was born in Savannah, Georgia and died in Nokomis, Florida. He lived in and out of orphanages until age sixteen – when he ran away to join the United States Merchant Marine. In eleven years of seamanship, he claimed he read a book a day and learned to write by typing out the complete text of *War and Peace* and editing out the errors – he subsequently threw the edited work in the ocean. Jessup was married to Vera in 1944 and had a daughter named Marina. He left the Merchant Marine in 1948 to become a fulltime author. He was at the typewriter ten hours a day.

His first novel, *The Cunning and the Haunted*, was published in 1954 and filmed as *The Young Don't Cry* in 1957. Three other novels were also adapted to film – *The Deadly Duo*, *Chuka*, and *The Cincinnati Kid*. He sold the movie rights to the 1971 novel *Foxway* but it was never filmed. Jessup published eleven novels – primarily westerns and spy thrillers – as Richard Telfair. His last novel, *Threat*, was published in 1981.

Jessup's obituary claims he wrote under multiple pseudonyms and published over sixty novels. At this time we can only confirm the pseudonym Richard Telfair and the existence of thirty-four published novels.

Bibliography

Written as Richard Jessup
1954 – The Cunning and the Haunted (The Young Don't Cry)
1955 – A Rage to Die
1956 – Cry Passion
1957 – Cheyenne Saturday
1957 – Comanche Vengeance
1958 – Long Ride West
1958 – Lowdown
1958 – Texas Outlaw
1959 – The Deadly Duo
1959 – The Man in Charge
1960 – Sabadilla
1960 – Night Boat to Paris
1961 – Chuka
1961 – Port Angelique
1961 – Wolf Cop
1963 – The Cincinnati Kid
1967 – The Recreation Hall
1969 – Sailor
1970 – A Quiet Voyage Home
1971 – Foxway
1974 – The Hot Blue Sea
1981 – Threat

Written as Richard Telfair
1958 – Day of the Gun
1958 – Wyoming Jones
1959 – The Bloody Medallion
1959 – The Corpse that Talked
1959 – The Secret of Apache Canyon
1959 – Wyoming Jones for Hire
1960 – Scream Bloody Murder
1960 – Sundance
1961 – Good Luck, Sucker
1961 –The Slavers
1962 – Target for Tonight

Film Adaptations
1957 – The Young Don't Cry
1962 – Deadly Duo
1965 – The Cincinnati Kid
1967 - Chuka

Made in the USA
Charleston, SC
08 November 2011